# TOP
# DOLL

**Also by Karen McCarthy Woolf**

An Aviary of Small Birds
Seasonal Disturbances

# TOP DOLL

## Karen McCarthy Woolf

dialogue
books

DIALOGUE BOOKS

First published in Great Britain in 2024 by Dialogue Books

10 9 8 7 6 5 4 3 2 1

A CIP catalogue record for this book
is available from the British Library.

Hardback ISBN 978-0-349-70345-9
Trade paperback ISBN 978-0-349-70346-6

Extract on page 60 from 'Gypsy Woman (La Da Dee)' by Crystal Waters; songwriters: Crystal Waters & Neal Brian Conway; lyrics © Universal Music Publishing Group, Warner Chappell Music, Inc.

Typeset in Caslon by M Rules
Printed and bound in Great Britain by Clays Ltd, Elcograf S.p.A

Papers used by Dialogue Books are from well-managed forests
and other responsible sources.

Dialogue Books
Carmelite House
50 Victoria Embankment
London EC4Y 0DZ

www.dialoguebooks.co.uk

Dialogue Books, part of Little, Brown Book Group Limited,
an Hachette UK company.

For Zoë

# OBITUARIES AS FOUND

A single bouquet of daisies

The last known photograph
on a steamship        swaddled in furs
an antisocial
       socialite, an enigmatic figure

attended round-the-clock
surrounded
by fine French dolls      antique dolls
private aides

Daughter of a scoundrel.    Notorious curmudgeonly

Her behaviour was strange
     She avidly monitored      Sotheby's

\*

     Huguette Clark     died aged 104
in 1928 she married

French dolls          since she was a girl

Huguette's father, Senator

                          William A Clark of Montana
began collecting

four galleries, 121 rooms, Turkish baths
a rotunda      a swimming pool, a thundering
pipe organ and
a Michigan woman          Anna Eugenia

                          *

     Huguette
     so fiercely private
spoke English with a French accent

In 1928 she married—

Gossip               arrived with a
retinue of servants
and rented          an entire floor
for the duration of the divorce

The dolls      French dolls
were housed in their own suite of rooms

                          a life lived in the shadows

                          *

Lady Liberty was Anna la Chapelle 17
her mother

Her 56-year-old father      was not afraid
to show his wealth

The family was
received by New York society
as robber baron Beverly Hillbillies

In her teens Huguette took dancing lessons
from Isadora Duncan

A whirl                    of Paris


When her sister died, it left a hole
Why she became a recluse is not known

A housekeeper kept the dolls' dresses
impeccably ironed

Everything stopped when her mother died

She lavished
        a fortune
        died with a taste for
exquisite French dolls      baronial homes
and solitude

*

The next 80 years are almost completely blank
Fortunately, the Russians never attacked

William Clark
                    worth over $3 billion in today's money
Second childhood?
God complex?
What about the ethics?

          She didn't want to go out. She didn't want
          to have beautiful things, no, no. She was a
          lovely, kind, giving lady, I feel really saddened

*

A 14-foot tapestry from the 16th century
said

It was intriguing.
          For a number of years
          she ate austere lunches

was known only as The Client

          She just wanted to be home
and play with her dolls
          The dolls were coveted—
extensive
                    immense

Despite her unpredictable behaviour, Huguette
willed her doll collection
            to speak publicly

a copper tycoon's daughter
                highly paranoid    half-sister
                    bubble of concealment
                    and seclusion
she spent millions  was a big buyer

On the other hand   the maids' rooms
                were plain and unadorned

*

On the top floor of 907, Fifth Avenue

an aspiring photographer
is focusing in particular

        an expert appraisal for the IRS
        on a significant collection of dolls

In addition   Mrs Clark owned
mansions, historic
appliances from 1915
carved plaster ceilings, dark wood panelling
& dolls      dollhouses

*

In recent years
her eyesight failed and her hearing was weak
she married  but the union dissolved
two years later        of non-consummation

at times
                she had been unwilling
                        to eat

A \$7 million violin found
in the reclusive heiress's wardrobe
said she weighed
all of 75 lb like somebody
                        out of a concentration camp


                                *

She purchased several Japanese
and even some unique      Barbie dolls

                she spent over \$3 million
on dolls
French dolls
                from the 19th century

She registered
under a fake name and even made
one of her lawyers speak to her
through a door
                        at the New York hospital

                                *

The door      said
        an expert on antique teddy bears and dolls
                said
        Mrs Clark's collection has been
                appraised

                in the millions

The door      said she owned
four Stradivari including The Virgin
and an 1882 painting by Renoir *In the Roses*


The door      said
The Great Depression      said
The newspapers said


Have a look at her self-portraits
Have a look at
her paintings of Japanese ladies
        they were beautiful
            or maybe they were Japanese dolls

            Her cherished dolls
                    her constant companions

# DOLLY

**907 Fifth Avenue, Apartment 8W**
*25 March 1991 9 a.m.*

Alors! Dolly is making specials photographies projects
it is officials. By orders of Infernal Revenues Officer.
Big bucks investigation – ridiculous! This Polaroid camera
is heavy, this nosey-parkers will have regrets.

Luckily Dolly is fully jointed, bisque, as Maman's protector
and first favourite she is artistic types if not painter
as is Maman copying also cartoons characters.
Our home is 907 Fifth Avenue, bests address! Architect

diagrammatique for penthouse luxury, almost in clouds
fluffy and ethereal tufting our rooftop floor.
Miss Ting she is making assistance, porqoui non?

Our little bébé pram it is crowded
with equipments. I press the shutter to make a foyer
this is the farthest interior, our edge of horizon.

## FOYER

A dark and wide chasm, your nostrils will inadvertently
twitch at the odour of undisturbed indoors, a ghost scent,
of intoxicating  perfume, Grace Kelly's Fleurissimo to be
exact, of stacks of paper, dust, of tinned sardines, a trace
of rotting flesh within. A small painting hangs on the wall
above a mahogany hall table with dainty, club feet. On top
a 17th-century carriage clock, a sundial face surrounded by
swirls of gilt, a golden cherub clasping a scythe. The painting depicts a window (it is the apartment at night), looking
out across Central Park down to a street dotted with lamp
posts that glow like fireflies. A table. A Japanese silk cloth.
Taxis. A signature in the right-hand bottom corner reads
                                                    Huguette Clark.


This is most farthest of our interior, our edge of horizon.
We are not here often. A camera is heavy in arms petits
I am 12 inches. Or if in sophisticate Europe, centimetres – thirty!
Dans le catalogue I am described as French composition.

Value Points: *Especially pretty bébé avec gentle expression*
– this is maximums accurate blurbs! And now The Gallery:
Miss Ting, regarde! We must step back! So many flirty
eyes to catch from glassy cabinets, glancing in our élites direction.

Ringlets, petticoats, bonnets, silk embroidered vests,
blousons, ruffles, immaculate lace collars,—everywhere cute
and Nineteenth Century before even Maman is to be

born on 9 June 1906! Gemini star signs, which is bests
Zodiac arrangement. But now we make photos shoots
most thrilling of drama, tears, sometimes also les liaisons sexy!!

## GALLERY

Herringbone parquet stretches before you, a wooden sea
arrowing out to double doors. It's at this moment you realise you're being watched. Hundreds of pairs of socketed
lids blink. A monkey automaton in a red felt jerkin and
a fez hat holds a pair of cymbals. Next to it are rows of
little cafe chairs, piled legs up, pointing at folded beach
parasols, stacked next to an arrangement of instruments –
a tiny harp, a minuscule violin. Your eyes travel along the
wood-panelled wall to a door, and if you squint, you can
see the corner of an ornate, cherry-wood desk at the foot
of which there is another at which sits a dreadlocked rag
doll in a waistcoat, bent over a leather-bound journal, a
long quill pen clutched in his brown fist.

Shhhhh! Our genius Général is working. Memoirs apparently!
Miss Ting says purple, Dolly thinks adorable mauve:
our wallpaper's scattered with bouquets of primrose
and violets! Actually we've maisons for all the family.

I am furnishing the schoolroom entirely.
Here sits Adele and her sailor friend Emile with a globe
and map full of places where Maman will never go
or take us: the Continent or even the Islands of Hebrides.

Where is Miss Ting? Outside we are shells, like beetles.
Insides, more empty. Delphine-Jumeau loses a tooth each week.
And we must make the operation. Zut alors!
She screams, but this pain is nothing more than un petit
idea! A breeze whistles through empty bellies and shrieks!
Moi? My porcelain skull was cracked. I needed shiny new hairs.

This was 1928. Roaring times and crash!  Now I have new hair
and a fine line spidery spidering almost invisible crack that crawled
up my chin. Condition: *generally* excellent. Mr Husband was cruel
to Dolly and Maman did not guess his oak was veneer.
Imagine! *Wax loss on left eyelid.* See how this spindly legged chair
in my boudoir is solid. Strong. Also those gilt frames on the wall?
On my dresser, you'll note the top is marble.
Quick! Before I tell of Le Docteur let's make a picture!

Shhh we must not Maman disturbs! Le Docteur
did fix me in Paris and all Barbies did make rages
in their stereos. One bébé threw her rattle from the pram.
To be quite honests the whole nursery behaviour
was hysterical as if to make maximums jealous rampage.
Always this poupée wanted to suck milk with Maman.

## BOUDOIR

A lady's bedroom, furnished in antique pieces of note. A heaped Louis Quinze marquetry dressing table with three oval mirrors. Under it is a doll-size replica on the parquet floor, with a little chair. At the foot of a dishevelled white and gold bed, upholstered in green silk damask is a chest, on top of which is a simple, wooden box, with a hinged lid, swung open. A blond doll rests against this lean-to. She wears a cream, lace dress, cinched at the waist, with long, leg-o-mutton sleeves. Her head is tipped to one side, glassy blue eyes frown at the camera. Her left hand is raised, blurry, and appears to be pointing to a door opening on to an en suite bathroom. In the gloom, a shadow of an old woman stooped in an oversized dressing gown.

Yes, she was still un bébé so Maman
said our  Lisette must prepare all the bottles just so!
This is before Lisette is dropped dead! Also our collars and bows
it was her job to press after the clean starching and steam iron.
Olden days business. Once she is making Dolly cross to frown.
See how this jade mantelpiece is not crowded?
As a joke we gave chère Lisette a miniature cow
from Dolly's house! Now I am explaining the Music Room
and also the Chapel. Voila! Maman was not best pleased.
But us dolls we say eyes for an eye,
a teeths for a teeth. Look! This upright antique
piano is a Waltershausen. A Grecian frieze
hangs above the matchstick lute. It is exquisites.  C'est vrai.
Dolly is sent to get fixed. She flew straight across the Atlantic.

Dolly must wait 30 years to fly across the Atlantic
First Class! This is PanAms 1960s. Ooh la la. I feel a rush
of breath. This booby next to me was soft flesh
not fragile like my porcelain cheeks.
If only poor Maman could have come, if only she was bisque
she would be hollow and happy like us.
Please note this moose head, Dear Guest. I ask
at take-offs why did we bring this Chatty Talkative?

*Cherry Blossom Lends a Charm*
*to Existence.* I am having this on my bureau.
In Paris it is considered très chic!
But we are using more each week. Le Général urges calm,
like a lake not a sea. What does he know?
He was not the one whose head was not on its neck.


No, he is having a big, woolly head on his neck
with ears that go deaf when I shush him
because he is speaking but saying nothings!
Alors! You see Les Plastiques in their discothèque
with a two-inch glitter ball? Everyone expects
the globe of Dolly. Let me speak you something.
It is not rocket mathematics. Ecoutez bien!
Maman's Mr Husband was tippling over the deck
like Martini from a cocktail glass! But now I speak of Paris!
On this flight, one Subordinate (servant class) tries to stuff
Dolly in the overhead locker, like a coffin, no air!
No light! Then I blink and she is embarrassed, she
and a Cabins Stewards glance nervously and laugh
then lift my head so I too can see the sun's fire.

Every cloud has a silvery line. Maman'll fire
this Subordinate when we get home. I'll bet
they are not speaking of this lady in *my* seat.
First Class. Chatty Talkative is down in the hold, ha ha!!
Now her *teeth* they are chattering. I admire
her stamina if nothing else. The least
I could do was to tell Maman of the letter.
You see Mr Husband made hush-hush enquiry
to sell us at Christie's Auction House!
As if! Mais this is how my pretty tête was broken.
On that day many years ago my head it spins and twists
like horses on the multicoloured carousel.
This abominable was no joker.
Poor Dolly! My skin is icing white bisque.

Poor Dolly, because I am utterly bisque
the surgery was a very delicate procedure.
My neck was in the hands of Le Docteur,
my nostrils sniffing the desk.
Mon Dieu! He was lifting Dolly's dress
and petticoats to check for splinters
and Dolly was dreaming on adhesive vapour.
I do not like his touch, this best specialist.

Presently I am under a young oak
and the leaves they glow like absinthe
in a crystal decanter, I see the light shake.
The grass is scratching the small in my back.
It is August nineteen sixties and hot with the glint.
I see a man of large person. I am naked.

I see Maman. I am a person. I am naked.
But I am not human skin. Maman's nipple
is peeping from her sheer kimono, a ripple
of breeze she is billowing silk
dragon's breath, scarlet, flickering.
In the air the flutter is jasmine, a little
also the scent of honeysuckle.
Sun shafts the man's muscled trunk.

My breast she is heavy heaving
and I am feeling a particular tingle
as the man he is kissing Maman's throat,
her shoulders, you would not believe
how he strokes with fingers
her long hair, then she is making moan.

Maman is making moan, she pulls his hair
long, hard. Mais non! Now the man I dream
is Mr Husband not the enchanted handsome
and I am shivering under the chandelier.
In the mirror I am seeing the derrière
of Mr Husband, it is a fat white dome
bright as the moon! Maman is delirium
with fear and we must make her torture
to end. Regarde! How she is writhing
and scratching with fingernails his pale back.
'Allez! Allez!' She is calling assistance.
Quick! We must pull the Chatty string.
Mr Husband was wearing only a moustache
stiff with wax and making belligerent

bellowing as the maximum belligerent
beast-pig. I did not like his noisy breath
and the way he was trying to make push-push
on top of Maman. Chatty says *I don't want
to go to bed yet.* Merde! Such impertinent
nastiness! This imbécile doll is not French
no, no! But this is how we must wrench
Maman from Mr Husband's most violet
passions. *Please change my dress.* Impossible
behaviours! What is this Chatty Talkative
knowing about love? Salope!
Dolly sounds the alarm! It says *May I have a taffy apple?*
Idiot! Mr Husband said he would surely give
her one if she didn't shut up!

This was the noises that woke Dolly up!
*Donnez-moi un bonbon! Je suis très jolie.*
I am come round on the workbench in Paris
and now this Chatty will never stop
chatting. *Je m'appelle, je m'appelle . . .*
Monsieur le Docteur fixed her to say *oui, oui*
and other sentences like *Je suis très gentille,*
as if any vinyl-face could ever be a proper
Frenchwoman! They are all sames!
There is such things as class
and breeding. This doll was born in a box
with only a record player slot and speaker.
Tell me is there anything more dégueulasse?

Dolly is fashioned of aristocrat stock.
Maman's Maman did know Dolly's maker.

Anna-Maman was bringing my maker
all the way from Aix-en-Provence
because he was most genius in all France.
He did fashion Dolly for Maman's beloved big sister
Andrée, who in our tragedy, did die from a fever
most miserably raging and violent.
Quelle horreur! This is when our residence
is nearly ten times more larger
than Maman's most splendid parkside
apartments in Manhattan. Vraiment.
Papa Le Senator was second only to a Rockefeller.
Ooh la la! Every day a whole train piled
with coals came just for warming la maison.
He was the most extravagant man in America.

This was America's most extravagant
miser! He is buying every objêt in the world:
the ballroom is papered with gold
leaf, each table leg and cabinet is elegance
itself, the walls are thick with Renaissance
paintings. *There's nothing can't be sold
or bought* mais son coeur is hard wood
and Maman is feeling such chilly distance.

Dolly is speaking these delicate histoires
for Maman because now she is shy
and does not hardly exit this acre of penthouse

ever since the bombings on Pearl Harbor.
Mais oui, we are living almost fifty
million years like this and Maman is recluse.

We are exclusive now Maman is recluse
and it is us dolls only who know
her most intimate thoughts and how
she eats sardine crackers and orange juice.
Maman and Mr Husband made decree absolute.
Maman anyway prefers the Flintstones
and our Housekeeper must make correct the video
recordings. And now her weights is reduced
to skeleton fashions. Mais poor Maman, this money
is a curse more terrible than the occult
of the gypsies. There is no child or lawyer
can be trusted not to try and make a funny
business, no love that is not spoilt
or ruined like a soggy biscuit in a saucer.

This rumour is storm in a saucer.
Of course Dolly will go to live in The Hospital.
Now we are moving and it is my responsible
to select all of les maisons and furnitures
and to ready each chosen doll for departure.
I am advising Maman on who is suitable.
It is Dolly who is caring if Maman is comfortable.
Everybody knows Dolly is most like a daughter.
The Stradivarius is selling for seven zillion dollars
and also for many more the Renoir.
Yet Dolly is not listed in the catalogue at Sotheby's.

Even Le Général does not know what follows
next or how long we will live outside for.
Our fate is uncertain, tomorrow a mystery.

# THE GENERAL

**907 Fifth Avenue, Apartment 8W**
*25 March 1991 9 a.m.*

THE GENERAL is seated at his doll-size cherry-wood bureau, nestled between a radiator and precariously piled stacks of Betamax videos, labelled in black marker with *Flintstones*, *Scooby Doo*, *Jetsons* followed by season numbers in brackets, alongside towers of back issues of *Paris Match*. Dolly and Miss Ting wheel the pram containing the Polaroid and several envelopes of film across the parquet into the study, with its ceiling-high American hardwood bookshelves lined with mint first editions. The slightly faded rag doll lifts his head, brushing a stray dreadlock from his eye, straightens his dicky bow, snaps his braces against his chest and clears his throat.

—To what do I owe the pleasure?—he asks, not rising to his feet.

—Me an' Dolly mek documentary animation an h'inventory of all doll and—Miss Ting announces.

—Instants quickie locations scouts! Polaroid continuities. Is two minutes!—Dolly interrupts.

—Can it wait?!—The General asks, sighing as he raises an eyebrow, and shaking his restless left leg, a habit he has when immersed in

his writings.—We've got the Oscars once again this evening and
the Sakura Festival—

—It is not big deals! Dolly butts in.—Quickie portraits for
posteriors and stuffs—

—Posterity.—The General corrects Dolly, glancing at Miss Ting's
pert behind, then acquiesces. —Very well, Mademoiselle Dolly, my
wish is your command, but first allow me to—

—Me nah know why yuh cyaan use typewriter which is quicker
instead of h'insist on goose fedder pen like yuh is Charles Dickens
himself.—Miss Ting interrupts.

—As I have said many times, my dear Miss Ting, the writer
accesses a different level of consciousness with the pen, places the
machine cannot ...

—An' anyway, wha' kinda secret is in dere yuh keep it so close to
yuh chest so??—Miss Ting leans forward as if to grab the diary.

—Exactement! Now, let's go!—Dolly exclaims, clapping her little
porcelain hands, we are having no times to wastes. Dépêche-toi
Miss Ting, allez!

## STUDY

The General is seated at his desk, his journal open, the quill pen resting in the inkwell. He is dressed in a pale, light denim shirt, with large ivory buttons and a pink bow tie. His trousers are a dog-tooth check, with matching braces. On top of this ensemble he wears a waistcoat, with a small white hanky in the top pocket. His brown cotton face is two shades darker than Miss Ting's; she is perched on his lap, squinting slightly as she peers across the table in a bid to identify the magazine peeping out from under his papers, which appears to be a copy of *Playboy*. Behind her a large grandfather clock's hands are poised at just a minute before 12. You can tell by the weak light from the north-east window that it is midday rather than midnight.

Miss Ting wants to take the photo again because it's not her best angle, she's not even looking at the camera. Dolly snatches it back out of her hands and blows on it to dry the emerging image, and the two look like they are about to box like the plastic kangaroos who live on the fourth shelf of the cabinet in the hall. Dolly snaps no, it is *sufficement*. Miss Ting kisses her teeth, but The General has already gone back to his papers, turning a large egg timer over as he begins.

# THE GENERAL

## From Sand Creek to Fifth Avenue via Sunset Strip
*Reminiscences & Recollections of General Obadiah*
*Louverture Little Rock Yellow Bird Junior the Second*

## A MEMOIR

Every man has his Nemesis. Each man his Muse. & Truth be enunciated, nothing is more egregious than the distinct sensation of being trapped within a situation utterly Outside of one's Own control. Imagine then, if you will, the Jaws of a vast, slobbering, Halitosis-ridden Beast clenching shut over one's Midriff so that for a moment the prospect of Corporeal division is less a possibility than it is a likely, numerical outcome. Consider this a baptism of sorts, where the purifying torrents of the Colorado coalesce to a waterfall of lukewarm Drool that sinks into the very fibre of one's Being. Inhale again that foul Breath, pungent as the aroma of steaming Donkey Dung as you ride strapped to an overburdened saddlebag with your Face directly in the wake of the Mule in Front's Behind.

That One could emerge from this experience stronger, more resilient & ready to battle another day is a Triumph not only of the Spirit but testament to dear ample-Bosomed Miss Bessie's estimable skills with needle, thread, thimble & dexterous Fingertips that did fashion this invincible Body. This rough & tumble, as it is euphemistically ascribed, was the way with Byron & Turk & Tommy & the much-esteemed Snooks,—for each Hound pricked its Ears up regardless. Each wagged its stink-wafting Tail with the same Mindless enthusiasm as had its Father & its Father's Father. And each loved nothing better than to grasp its Master's competing Object of Desire in its blackening Gums and hide it under a bushel, as if my rag-stuffed Frame were no more sentient than a TableLeg. & Yet, Truth be articulated, there was no creature, of two Legs or four, to whom Young Junior was more devoted.

But more of Master William Clark the Second, patron, bon viveur & half Brother to our Maman & his wretched, spittle-spouting Canine Snooks in due course. Now I ask, dear Friend, that you close your Eyes & allow the ripple of your Thoughts to wander, back along a dark & treacherous path, that I might account for the whats & whereabouts of my arrival, here in this ample yet limited apartment. Open your Ears & listen out for the Whistle & Shout of Frontiers Men & Fur Trappers who followed in the moccasin-clad Footsteps of those who knew the Songs & Stories of hard earth and prairie grass. To a place of snow-capped peaks & eucalyptus campfires; of sage fields, cacti, creeks & caverns; where Men of Soft-Flesh, White-Skin & Little Scruple came to plunder our gracious Mother Earth's seemingly infinite bounty.

Cast your Mind back to that most *uncivil* War, when the rape & ransacking of the West was rudely interrupted by a battle between North & South, which despite its pretensions to a nobler cause, was in reality no more than one White-Flesh vying with another for constitutional supremacy. More of that heresy later, for I know there are those who would bid me write these facts more grateful, as if Emancipation were the starry flag that set the course, when in reality us Enslaved, whether cloth or Flesh, were no true priority for neither Yank nor Rebel.

It is to these Blood-drenched days, of muddy fields & cavalry where my provenance on this earth began. It was in those times of whisky-fuelled saloon bar bordello brawls where Flesh bought Flesh on auction blocks for little more than a Hog-Skin purse of dusty gold, that I, General Obadiah Louverture Little Rock Yellow Bird Junior the Second did first catch sight of this topsy-turvy world through my own Ivory-Eyes. A world when Fate & her brazen Nymphes, whose Dance is a shimmering in perpetual night, changed the course of my Existence. For it was in this lengthy & degraded political era that I was fashioned, gifted & thieved, falling eventually into the ever-grasping Hands of the Patriarch & soon-to-be Senator of Montana, William Clark, whose Appetite for ore – whether, gold, silver or copper – was outshone only by what he was willing to do in order to acquire it.

But afore we come to acquaintance with that nefarious politician & Father to his own clan of wayward Offspring, let us journey back through the decades, to another century, to the era in which it all began—to a time of whimsy & witness, of hard truth & uncertain imagination . . . to a young Girl, whose fortune it was to have me, Obadiah Louverture Little Rock Yellow Bird Junior the Second, as her Mannequin-Companion & whose misfortune it was to be born Black Flesh a few degrees south of the line where servitude gave way to iron Collars & Cuffs, Bloodhounds & Auction Blocks.

§

*Virginia. Summer 1860. The Pryce Family Smallholding.*
Eliza lies down at the edge of the River, a pair of Dragonflies hovering between the indolent Arms of a willow stroking the water's surface, the gentle incline of the grassy bank somehow reassuring in its pressure on the small of her Back, which throbbed, as did her left Temple. She closes her Eyes – or to be exact her right Eye, for the left was puffy & barely opened a Slit. Why, she wondered, did they call it a black Eye, when the Bruise was as rainbow-hued as the inside of the Oyster Shells they used to pluck from the beds of the Rappahannock?

The breeze is cooler now, the sun sinking lower in the sky and Eliza can Hear the aggravated scrape of Obadiah's hoe on the stony, uncooperative ground that constituted the Walled Garden as Mistress Pryce liked to call it. Or was it Pierce? Pryce, Price, Rice. It was a long time ago & Memory's clouds can gather & obscure, filmy as Cataracts. Rows of carrots, eggplant, cabbage, sweet & Irish potatoes were out of sight from the porch, or veran-dah, or lah-di-dah, as Hannah, Eliza's mama used to call it, & thus its yield was sorely compromised by a gnarled tangle of Thirsty tree roots and lack of light. This diminished fecundity did not concern the Myopic and somewhat infirm Lady of the Smallholding; or rather it did, only in that The Patch, as the inhabitants of the Cabin called it, was for her an emblem of the family's unbridled generosity & modern approach to that barbaric & increasingly contested economic institution which was causing consternation across the land. Did this Philanthropy not distinguish her & Mister Roderick from those vulgar, more commercially minded Planter-Flesh on the other side of the mountains, where Little Black Flesh that could scarcely Crawl never mind Walk were left to forage on their Knees for

Grasshoppers to fling on the fire & scavenge in the Cow shed amongst Shit-smeared Hogs for forgotten cobs of corn?

Do not think I exaggerate, dear Friend, these deprivations are documented & in some Philistine quarters even met with celebration & relish. There are little bounds, it appears, to what one Soft-Flesh might concoct & enact upon another for the most trivial &, conversely, the most profound, material advantage.

It is July already, Spring having concluded & summer arrived with as little ceremony as a Donkey's Fart. The Bewhiskered Man with coffee Breath from the Government had also been & departed. Eliza Brown (14) has been itemised & identified by Gender & moon cycles but not named in the household inventory. As has her Mamma (Hannah, 30), Grandmammie (Bessie, 46), Father (Obadiah, 37), & Son (John, 1) who although also nameless, was rendered distinct by the appellation Mulatto. Also listed is a boy, 16 (Isaac) and his sister Marie-Louise (12) and Jerome (30) who is like a father to the pair, not by Flesh-Blood but by circumstance, for they were young & still fat-Fingered when they were sold on from their Flesh-Folk & he had clutched Eyes with their Mother through her screams & Snot-riddled Tears & nodded in silent assent, so as she would know he would *look out for them*. They had all three arrived as a 'job lot', in payment of a recreational wager – or, to phrase it more bluntly, they had been won at cards on a chilly winter's night by the Pryce's son Billy, who had not yet settled on any appropriate Female-White-Flesh & was busy with his Friends sowing their oats, wheat & barley about the place, Willy-Nilly.

The arrival of a new Motherless family two years whence had caused quite a stir in the Cabin, which hitherto had been occupied solely by the Browns who were now bidden to accommodate a clutch of absolute Strangers into their already crowded quarters. What followed was a long, drawn-out & futile battle for territory that in truth did not exist – for at any moment, and it had been proved time and time again, what little the White-Flesh gave with one Hand (old blankets for patchwork quilting, candle stubs with half-buried and unignitable wicks) they snatched back with the other.

Not being named in that inventory had its advantages though & Obadiah had carried the bestowed name Brown with him from Alabama where he had been born & sold & Hannah & Eliza had taken it too. Thus it was, that Eliza's naming her son John – hardly an imaginative moniker at first glance – was an aspirational manoeuvre, for the little Mite was named after none other than Old John Brown, leader of the thwarted Raid at Harpers Ferry.

Brown was White-Flesh, abolitionist & his plan to raid the military arsenal at that strategic point where rivers, state lines & railway tracks collided was audacious as Hell. Hell, however, pre-vailed on this occasion, & the idealistic, some would say gung-ho Brown, along with his brave brigade, was surrounded, captured, slashed in the Neck by a sabre that narrowly missed his Crown & hanged for treason & murder in December 1859, shortly after the revolt earlier that Fall, in which two of his Sons had perished.

It was the sacrifice of his own Soft-Flesh & Blood that had so inspired Eliza, for there were divided opinions in the cabin as to the purity of Brown's motives. Grandmammie Bessie believed the authenticity of his piety was compromised as a White-Flesh that can never, *ever*, be trusted & that his recklessness put the Lives of volunteer Black Flesh Folk at risk. EveryBody knew it was a plan that Mr Frederick Douglass himself had resisted, declining to join Brown's band of Insurgents as it was plain as a working day in a tobacco field is long that this was a Hare-Brained & predictably fatal scheme that could end in nothing but tragedy & disaster. Eliza had countered that the very fact he was White-Flesh proved the sincerity of his intentions, for in the material scheme of it he had less to gain from Emancipation.

Hannah had Sighed, a deep, resigned & lengthy Sigh, that said, unequivocally *there's no use talking to her when she gets like this, that Girl has hard Ears & a Mind more stubborn than Solomon's Mule who took his time lugging barrels of bourbon over the hill, no matter what carrot was dangled, no matter which whip lashed his Bloody, fly-infested Flank*.

Obadiah had said nothing, as was his way, though it was obvious to any alert observer, from how he shook his good Knee & Frowned the whole time Eliza was talking, that he agreed, Whole-Heartedly, with Bessie when she'd snapped that she couldn't fathom *why on God's Earth Eliza didn't name the Mewling Brat after her own Father as was customary for a Firstborn and be done with it?* Eliza then took it upon her Self to jab back with a hasty & ill-advised retort, saying she'd named the Rag Doll Grandmammie Bessie had stitched for the Little-Un 'O-ba-diah' already, thank you very much, the name was taken & she'd be the One, the *only* One to decide on who her Son was named from.

At this point Obadiah hoiked up his dungarees, Spat his tobacco on to the ground, cast a disparaging Glance at his emphatic Daughter & left the room. It was a dignified exit, if undermined by the ferocity of Hannah's attack, which was swift as it was unexpected. She struck her Daughter, hard & in the Face with a Cry that was at once wounded & warlike. That my rag-stuffed Physique was the sturdy implement with which Hannah made her blow should have softened the impact. But, Alas, my right Button-Eye caught the Bone of Eliza's Cheek & the damage was done. Bone against Bone. & It was then Eliza's turn to snatch me up from the floor, as if my retrieval were a matter of grave importance & dash out from the room, leaving the now agitated Babe in the Arms of Grandmammie Bessie, who rocked & shushed little John, for indeed that was his name, until his bawling subsided.

& So we find Eliza Brown, pensive & petulant, down at the edge of the River, in her Spot, that place she likes to prevaricate & ponder & suck the little sweet out of a stalk of grass. This was the same, exact Spot where she had been, that time, that One Time, a year ago, when Cousin Tom, as he liked to call himself, though he was Cousin nor Uncle to none, had surprised her, popping up out of nowhere like a Punchinello in a seaside theatrical, a Gleam in his Eye, his Head Cocked inquisitively to one side.

*Penny for your thoughts.* That was what he had said & she had not answered, merely turned her Head, ever so slightly in his direction. Not as encouragement, but so as to avoid a Punitive, the lash perhaps, or some form of confiscation or deprivation of provisions, for which the whole cabin would be aware of & made to jointly suffer. You see, those days it was considered quite some insolence for any Black Flesh to ignore a direct address from any White-Flesh. Equally, it was a regular & unpredictable danger to interact.

*My, that's a pretty Dress.* That was what he had said, as he plonked himself down beside her, placed his Hand that shook a little from last night's whisky, lightly, on her Limb, above the Knee & just below the Thigh, & pressed it ever so slightly so it sent a shiver, writhing like an Adder up her Spine.

It was a memory & a nightmare all in one, that came & went, in vivid violets, yellows & greens, the colour of the nausea, that arrived mornings, when she woke a good two hours before

Cock-Crow, a film of sweat on her Forehead & a beading on her Top-Lip, to see Grandmammie's Ribcage, rising & falling in time to her quiet yet perpetual Snoring. & It was these images that kept her awake, Night-times, when she lay on her Side to accommodate the weight of her distended Belly & the burgeoning Flesh-Foetus within.

*That's a good Girl, just relax.* This was what he had said, as he cupped her Lips with his Palm that reeked of cigarettes & onions & Horses. *You'll soon be back in the Saddle.* This is what he had said, once he had shuddered & twitched & released his effluence inside her.

# DOLLY

**907 Fifth Avenue, Apartment 8W**
*25 March 1991 12.12 p.m.*

Dolly doesn't like visiting Barbieville. Not through fear or trepida-tion, but simply because she considers it to be beneath her. Beneath any porcelain. The Barbies are a fact of life, yes, but their purpose, their necessity, as far as she is concerned, is debatable at best. They are mass manufacture and individuality is an alien concept. Their characteristics are predefined and if not stereotypical then perhaps more charitably, one might call them iconic. The Barbie Hive-Mind is a collective entity and like an ocean-going liner it is hard for them to alter their course.

—Dem a tek good picture tho, yuh mus admit, eh?—Miss Ting always has sight of the positives, even if at times her demeanour says otherwise.—Oonoo cyaan say dem nah photogenics. And DJ Kenny Ken an' im crew look good in those tight denims, eh, Miss Dolly? Me did see yuh sneak a peek at those rippling pecs!—

—Putaines! Les touts.—Dolly swings her head around, as if she's heard a scampering behind her as the two dolls cross the diagonal of the gallery towards the corridor which opens out onto the out-skirts of the brightly coloured, plastic citadel. Her instinct is on point: a red Ferrari zooms past with Italian Barbie at the wheel, and she waves a *Ciao! Bellas!* and toots her horn, veering sharply around the corner. She is parked up at the arched gates of the villa when they arrive.

—Allora! Miss Ting! Como estai?—she calls, nodding briefly at Dolly, pushing back her sunglasses onto her smooth forehead.—You wanna take a photo?—

## THE VILLA

A turquoise satin coverlet sits atop a plush Queen divan around which a gang of Barbies sip Mai-Tai's under parasols. Flush against the headrest behind them is a white mansion, and opposite under the onyx mantelpiece there's a crescent of dollhouses, one with the facade removed, exposing a warren of bedrooms, a kitchen, with dishwasher, Moulinex Etc and upstairs a bathroom where Scientist Barbie dressed in a lab coat, suspenders and plastic goggles lights a cigarette with a Bunsen burner as her assistant holds a fluorescent pink test tube up to the light. At the foot of the stairs, by a desk with a cash register, a Barbie in a one-piece leans back on a chair, a large cellphone pressed to her ear, a little black felt cat weaving around her slender ankles.

# CEO BARBIE

As a Senior Business Professional I'm never without my
briefcase even at the beach! My polka dot bikini & cerise

cravat tied in a pussy-bow tucks between the lapels of my
double-breasted power suit & my glossy stare    A Chief

Executive must know    how to delegate!   I told Dolly:
fax me darling! I'll have my people look right into it    Crack the

glass ceiling? Sure!   I'm vintage 1985, a ball breaker, obviously
head hunted, Cherry Blossom that's my brand   This is my

itinerary:      breakfast briefing, let's do lunch!  My dream
job is Right Now!  My desk faces the door    Feng Shui says

killer heels should be sharp & pointed as a  You're fired! memo
Luck isn't relevant in business!  Or politics  They're governed by

market forces!   Before Maman got real sick  Dolly
negotiated a crazy deal  with our head of production  I was

obliged to overrule in the same way my role model  Nancy kept
President Reagan in check! I mean everyone agrees his IQ was

questionable, his PR skills slightly better   He even angled
ROI    on the Iran-Contra affair!    There's money in arms

sales but drugs  are so much more effective   in the long
term, particularly when you declare War on them:   gear's

ubiquitous     as shoulder pads    All Dolly wants is a
VIP guest list    while I keep my head down under my

wide-brimmed hat  Our business plan involves a lot of
Xanax   which was big back then! Anxiety is through the roof

year on year     I took a lot from my corporate  Bible: Sun
Tzu's *Art of War* It says *strike the weak!* Just like Ron & Nancy

Next stop is Japan Town, a place which exerts its own timescales
via its multiple layers of ritual and decorum. It is by far the best
situated environment, with airy views across Central Park. It
boasts two windows facing west, under which are housed various
exquisite lacquerware sideboards replete with numerous jade vases
and ornaments that flank the Emperor's summer and winter pal-
aces. All around the room hang portraits of white-visaged ladies,
in elaborate, peach- and plum-coloured kimonos, decorated with
cranes, peonies and chrysanthemums.

Two Imperial Guards of the Shōwa era stand at the threshold.
An abundance of natural light streams onto the peach and cherry
orchards which flourish with fragrant blossom in spring. In winter

chestnut roasters gather around the ornate pewter fireplace and noblemen gather to brag of concubines and drink sake. An exactly to scale Kabuki Theatre with gable roof is positioned perpendicular to the hearth around which sit various performers wearing upswept topknots and decorative combs, their lilac and emerald crepe silk costumes bathed in early afternoon light.

Dolly explains the nature of their business to the elder Gofun-faced guard, keeping her eyes trained, fastidiously away from the orchards, while Miss Ting flirts and drinks a thimbleful of green tea that looks suspiciously like sake with the other. Normally, one would have a written invitation to a tea ceremony with Lady Mamiko in her elegant script, but today they are having to rely on their wits. They may enter, but the Empress has forbidden all photography, they must leave the camera at the gate.

The two dolls make their way across the fine silk Chinoiserie carpet in silence, passing by many more minor and historically exact buildings which house the major families of Court, momentarily lost in their own thoughts and glad to be rid of the Polaroid which is heavier than expected. Dolly remarks that she should have brought Delphine-Jumeau or another of the porcelains to help them carry it and Miss Ting nods.

They walk out past the Gallery again, as the lack of internal connecting door is the one notable architectural defect. Here, crammed together in the top cabinets are the servant class, whose job it is to attend and service the aristocrats who reside within. As the dolls enter the dining room adjacent, we find the bonsai nursery spread out under the mahogany table fashioned from numerous miniatures of these diminutive trees. Tucked between the fireplace and the single south-facing window are the discrete, screened apartments of Lady Mamiko and her most favoured lover, the Lady of the Bonsai, whose padded red silk robes indicate her to be a Maiko, or apprentice Geisha.  A pair of white doves have roosted above the windowsill, and can be heard, Lady Mamiko informs them as they arrive, cooing at dusk.

She offers tea, which they accept, and suggests a renga, which they do not. Lady Mamiko's sigh of relief is almost imperceptible, as she hands them a scroll each as invitation to the Sakura festivities. It is very diligent of Dolly, she adds as they depart, making sure everything is present and correct, as she continues with her preparations to accompany Maman to the hospital. Despite the polite chitter chatter, she seems tired, and keen to get back to her calligraphy in the garden.

# LADY MAMIKO

**907 Fifth Avenue, Apartment 8W**
*25 March 1991 2 p.m. Sakura Season*

> How long the days last.
> Long as the shadows in the hall.
> Long as Hikaru's hair.

Madame Huguette our Maman visits constantly these days. Sometimes she gets lost because there are many rooms and many doors, some with mirrors and even though she is the architect of our citadel and aware of every detail, age is oblivious and exacts its price. This means that Maman has been known to fall asleep while peering down into the Imperial Courtyard from above, her chin bobbing to the wishbone on her chest as she takes notes and measurements in her red leather book.

This morning was hardly convenient. No sooner had the porcelains ushered Maman home to their land of ringlets and petticoats before she shuffled back at dawn to rearrange the table settings for the Sakura Festival. As if I had not considered this and all the intricacies of rank which I have explained many times. It was a miracle she didn't trip and gash her forehead. Her eyesight is almost as bad as her hearing. There is also the smell, which is pungent. Nonetheless I must receive her with all due decorum, as here I am both guest and host.

> My shoulders glisten
> when Prince Hikaru comes—then leaves
> just before sunrise.

The art of diplomacy must be unseen and is therefore often undervalued. When Maman arrives with her cardigan on inside out I compliment her on her calligraphy and the authenticity of the tilework on the Temple Roof. This makes her smile, which is less than pleasant these days. Nonetheless, it elicits the desired effect, for she often wanders back to the library to fetch more paper and ink so she can draw a new scene for her latest kabuki production or anime. On a good day this journey can take up to an hour.

> There are many doors
> in Chrysanthemum Castle
> and dark passages.

Last time Maman's only surviving friend Madame P telephoned our Housekeeper answered. In her rush to pick up the receiver after the twenty-ninth ring she absent-mindedly left a window in the study ajar. The General was annoyed because it ruffled his papers. That was September, and now it's March. One could not blame a Housekeeper for failing to close the window. There are twenty million windows, some with park views. Then a week after Thanksgiving the poor thing caught a cold which was soon pneumonia, a common condition amongst the elderly. This was nothing to do with the open window. There was no disruption to her routine. She came and went, arriving at seven-thirty and leaving at the exact same hour to catch the subway home to Parkchester in the Bronx. Her infection came from outside. No one was surprised when the telephone rang again. Maman was kind and of course paid for the funeral and flowers. But a new Housekeeper means a stranger, and Maman does not like strangers. She will do almost anything to avoid them.

> Some cherry petals
> look like pink
> snowflakes from afar.

I liked it when the window was open. You could hear police sirens on the street below and geese honking as they flew past. It was chilly, but also magical, particularly at night.

> So many moons pass
> while Shining Hikaru sleeps
> with his concubines.

Two men came to deliver the Christmas Tree and Maman watched from behind the living room door. You could tell they were surprised to see so many of us gathered together in the Gallery. One of them asked to use the bathroom and to get to a guest toilet he had to walk along the corridor where the porcelains have their chairs. He did not spend much time in there. When he came out he glanced quickly down the dim hallway and wrinkled his nose, trying to place the aroma of rancid flesh. When he saw we were watching he hoiked up his jeans which hung so low as to reveal a slightly hairy stomach and hurried towards the foyer. His counterpart was peering at a small watercolour and seemed about to unhook it from the wall when Maman appeared. He jumped, almost knocking over an enamel vase of the Edo period that lived on the hall table. I found it amusing. Dolly was outraged. Miss Ting too. Maman's eyesight is no longer sharp but her timing was fortuitous as it was accidental, for Maman would never have appeared in front of the deliverymen had she not been so disorientated. Anyway, that vase was lonely and unloved. So much moral outrage about a theft that didn't even happen.

> All the china dolls
> are becoming a nuisance
> now blossom is scarce.

> One crawled underneath
> the porch at twilight—scrabbling
> with chipped fingernails.

Privacy is also in short supply. Maman is very rich so she always wins at auction. A new doll arrives, often a porcelain, sometimes a Barbie, and Dolly becomes agitated and fierce. I thought she would have learnt by now that Maman's attention span is brief and becoming briefer. The novelty wears off and within a week the new doll must take her place as a commoner amongst her kin. Otherwise Maman is busy here in Japan Town, if not reading, or painting or devising new quadrants in which to house us, we are rehearsing. Ever since Maman saw the *Tale of Genji* animation she has been in love with Hikaru. So much so she is eager to overlook many imperfections in his character.

A nobleman boasts
of every bud he splits.
How very noble.


Maman is innocent when it comes to love and marriage which is often a pragmatic arrangement. If Mr Husband was frustrated by Maman's trepidation he was happy with his million dollars. At least that's what Dolly says. She was here when it all happened. It paid for many gin slings in speakeasy bars, mink coats and a honeymoon with a gaudy new wife on the French Riviera. Dolly is myopic in her loyalties, but I think she may be right.


A lady's skin shines on
on moonlit pillows—soft and
quietly yielding.


I prefer to keep my Lady of the Bonsai to myself. Our time together is snatched between endless rehearsals with Hikaru.


Genji comes again
and now he expects me to
wait—patiently!


Hikaru Genji takes it all very seriously. Or, he takes himself very seriously. There is a lot of strutting and sweeping his hair from his eyes. I cannot deny he is handsome though it's also true that when he leans in to kiss me for the twentieth time my mind tends to be elsewhere.

His morning after
poem took longer than I thought
to go up in flames.


It is quite thoughtless
to write to me of bonsai—
My Lady's passion!

Our Lisette is gone now and for this reason I'm having to make do with last year's confetti. Luckily the Emperor is easily distracted by eyelashes, long white necks and the prospect of sake.

—Sooner than be a man, I'd be a sake jar, soaking in sake.— That is the Emperor quoting the poet Ōtomo no Tabito. He loves his sake. And quoting poets, as if he were the only one to have read them.

—That would be lovely for sake jars, and sake, Your Majesty—I tell him—but unlike those men whose poems are written and quoted at tea ceremonies centuries later, my vocation is to attend to demands and desires beyond my own—He raises an eyebrow at this, as he fishes for the compliment, which is gasping like koi for a little air at the surface of the pool, obvious and necessary. The Empress, who has been staring out of the window listlessly up to this point, turns to face me.

—And what of the bonsai orchards? Hikaru tells me the porcelains have been seen foraging before dawn.—

—Before dawn?—I echo in a bid to gain a moment to collect my thoughts. Does the Empress know I have been entertaining Hikaru at night? How can she not know? It is a little kept secret that keeps the gossip away from where my heart really lies. After all, Maman does require that Hikaru and I rehearse. Endlessly.

—Yes.—The Empress snaps, with a force that exceeds her usual passion for the subject.—Surely we shan't have to make do with last year's petals again?—

—Of course not Your Highness!—It's not exactly the truth but what else might I say? My Lady cannot keep up with production and the Barbies drive a hard bargain. Yesterday Japanese Barbie came to tell me that if I want blossom stocks for our Sakura festivities we will need to act quickly. It is Oscars night and the porcelains will be distracted, now is the time to strike. How ironic. Having to contemplate a raid to get back a thing that was stolen from you in the first place. Blossom was a mistake. Not the craze itself, although that is definitely a mistake, but the discovery of its side effects. In Japan Town we grow petals on bonsai, we have confetti from Macy's; we have no use for powder.

> A crow's caw is rough
> and not at all musical
> though they too like to sing.

# MISS TING

**907 Fifth Avenue, Apartment 8W**
*25 March 1991 4 p.m.*

Miss Ting says she's tired and wants to take a nap before the
evening, but Dolly persuades her to sit for a portrait at home, so
she pours them both a glass of sarsaparilla to drink on the verandah. Dolly, never one not to fill a silence, however companionable,
remarks how she finds it quite *extraordinaries* how in Jamaica they
also have television. Miss Ting rolls her eyes, spurred into action
by irritation.

—Come nuh Dolly—let's do this portrait business before
this likkle rag doll Miss Ting nods off to sleep an' start snore.
Mi have nuff tings fi do roun' di house, and remember mi did
promise di General fi mek saltfish fritters fi 'im dinner, since it's
Friday.—Dolly presses the shutter and moments later a Polaroid
print duly emerges from the long, slit mouth of the camera. Miss
Ting snatches the print from Dolly's hand and flutters it in front
of her face like one of the Andalusian fans splayed out on her
sideboard, where a cream dial telephone also sits. She inspects the
photo forensically as the image appears, frowns and rips it into
pieces. After she's rearranged the green glass vase with everlasting,

miniature carnations, repositioned the crochet shawl to reveal her shoulders, straightened the silk purple cloth over her tarot pack, added a peacock feather, checked her nails and reapplied her lipstick, she nods in assent. Dolly steps back off the edge of the Persian, pre-Islamic carpet dancing with fawns in a forest, holds the camera to her eye and presses the shutter again. As she hands Miss Ting her second attempt, the cream telephone rings. Both dolls jump, though it's nothing out of the ordinary.

Miss Ting makes her excuses to Dolly, it's her cousin Sherry from Birmingham, UK, she always calls at this hour, and tucks the receiver under her chin, while she sees Dolly to the front door. The telephone conversation that ensues is a series of pronouncements, punctuated by intermittent *uh–huhs*.

Miss Ting

did leave Jamaica July nineteen heighty-one, same month as Charles 'n' Di Royal Wedding extravaganza Dolly glue er two-blue-glass-eye pon like cat watch birdie wit di rest ah dem fool-fool h'Uptown por-ce-laine fancy. Miss Ting nah ooh an aah h-over no blondie-fairy-tale princess wid side-eye H'attitude same way nuff ah di Barbie-dem ah look pon di General. H'evrybody ah love off Lady Di an' buy cup n saucer n teatowel tuh prove it, but me, Miss Ting, nah trust er far as mi could throw er in er diamond tiara n see-tru skirt blow up inna de wind show er panty-dem by what newspaper call H'accident.

If Miss Ting

wan catch h'attention she lif up er frilly red ruffles wit er h'own two han an flash er thigh-top n pumpum quick like lightnin then toss er head back same way Brazil Barbie flirt wit Salsa Sindy pon chequerboard disco dancefloor. H'anyway, me ask yuh, what di royal famlee h'ever do fuh Jamaica-people cept come lock off we beach when dem sail in pon Royal Yacht Britannia? Choa.

Miss Ting

nah curtsey pon bended knee unless it di Queen of h'Englan 'erself require it! Even den Miss Ting go tink bout it firs'! Is Miss Ting great-great-great-granny did come from up innah di Blue Mountain an 'er headscarf was ah scrap offa Nanny h'own. Is di same patch from Nanny ceremonial garment on Miss Ting bed quilt. Is same spirit ah h'adventure run tru this Jamaica rag doll's stitches, same talawa maroon no man cyan forget when 'im gaze pon Miss Ting's slender neck an' button-eye wherever mi h'end-up. Mi nevah did h'ask fi Nurse Gwen fi bring mi fi live up innah New York, Queens, Jamaica h'Avenue. Uh-uh. Even if me h'affi come America is still *Jah-maica h'Avenue* dem ah bring me. Yuh hear dat? Jah-maica. Same way mi nah go coo-coo, ooh aah over Japan-Cherry tree like turtle dove when Miss Ting siddung under pink n purple poui-poui ah catch breeze in er own pretty garden while nightingale sing sweet romantic melody of an evenin. Nah sir. It cyaan run no way other than that.

Miss Ting

did hear how Nurse Gwen did carry 'er cross town an' leave 'er inna lawyer h'office in Manhattan skyscraper lie down in likkle basket like baby Moses pon di Nile river bank as tank-yuh present fi di h'ole lady who gift er thirty-thousan' dollar. US. Thirty thousan' dollar was nuff money dem days, an di joke is Nurse Gwen did tink it was tree-hun'red dollar which h'even so was a nice piece a change. Nurse Gwen no know no Missus C from Fift h'Avenue pent'ouse. She did look aftah a h'elderly fellah mek im money pon Wall Street an apparently is Missus C money 'im invest good. Is 'er daughter look pon di cheque Missus C lawyer did give er an' see all dem extra Os. Then is 'er mouth gape like goldfish blow bubble in glass bowl O, O so.

Is Miss Ting

did first notice Missus C start get mahga long before she catch carcinoma-nasty. Dis one reason nuff a di Barbie nyam off Cherry B powder. Yuh nah goh fatten up on cherry. An if Maman ah go look mahga di Barbie dem will wan' go skinny too-too cos h'everybody know dem mus' follow flesh-fashion. Is the way a di doll world. H'evry doll 'n' teddy live under same roof must abide by this rule n reg. An' is for this reason Scientist Barbie cyaan keep up wid supply n demand. When Dolly go pressure er fi powdah fi mek paste fi Missus C nuff a dem Blossom Barbie a hustle fi by-product. Next ting yuh know by-product nuah extra, is de ting itself. Miss Ting ah tell di General dis nuah run good, when chicken merry hawk de near.  On this h'occasion look like di General go turn ram goat wid all a di Barbie ready fi jump an wine pon im h'evry time 'im set foot inna Barbieville discotheque. An' cos General G spen' so much years wit Maman's big brother Uncle B-J h'inna Los H'Angeles petting party villa Pastor say is Sodom an' Gomorrah to the max 'im nah have strength fi resist di call ah di Barbie pumpum h'each an every time.

Miss Ting begin to think Scientist Barbie an 'er crew wuk science pon 'im but truth be tole leopard nah change 'im spot. Why eat likkle sprat pon roadside when yuh can nyam curry lobster a yuh yard? Dis a question Miss Ting h'ask di General pon nuff h'occasion but 'im jump like 'im have nuff h'ants down 'im pants an' tell mi 'im affi go out pon road mek a move and help *Mademoiselle* Dolly wid Special Undercover Operation Cherry. Las' time Miss Ting buck up on 'im headin from di direction a Barbieville Disco 'im nah look 'er inna di eye an 'im carry new fob watch in 'im waistcoat pocket. Dolly, she tink General G come fi find er fi special friendship. Choa.

Miss Ting did notice how di General's new watch nice an' shiny so an' when 'im tink se she nuah look, 'im tuck di gold chain inside it an tink se she nuah go see it deh so. An' di General not even a Jamaican bredrin. Him wear short locks an' preach Jah-Jah Wisdom but when 'im play selectah back to back with DJ Kenny Ken and Don Selecta who sport wet-look Jerry-curl afro, is Shabba Ranks Trailer Load an Mister Lover Man 'im play while di Blondie Barbies dem writhe like centipede up an' down pon shiny disco pole.

Is then that me, Miss Ting did feel a shiver of prediction tremble tru 'er gold hoop earrings that jangle above 'er shoulders wheneva she tosses her head.

# MOSCOW BARBIE

America does not like Russian though    they love to eat
borscht in Brooklyn   I am best   ice skater   in all

Central Park    & most fast  They try to keep up I say
*dosvedanya!*    twirl trim on my muff    It is most

expensive muff! Then I am off!   Miss Ting   tries to
freeze   Tatiana out   Big Mistake    This cannot make

General-G    give Tatiana up  Tatiana survives  Siberia in
halter-top       When I smile   it is enough   to crack

ice on frozen lake   so I can dip   tootsies  to swim in
January  Tatiana  was most popular   dinner date in all

Kremlin       She is driving  Mercedes  while First Lady sit in
Lada!  It is not matter of debate if Tatiana   has lover in

Moldova       bendy as acrobat in Moscow State Circus
*Niet!*  whenever I say this word   my General says Yes!

Oligarchy     is traditional system followed by Maman's Papa
*Perestroika*  with copper pennies and wires     Why  ask

question  if answer is obvious?  Better to toss blondie
ringlets, flutter eyelash   eat Beluga caviar   while it lasts

Spy Master was Soviet option now everyone has information
technology job   For small thing   Dolly rips off head

Undercover work is dangerous    Spirit of *glasnost*  is in
vodka martini  Rum punch?  I am iron fist in steel glove

with soft spot for pussy  cat Muschkin  so cute!  Hotel
Excelsior  has best suite for photographer to jump out   Or on

yacht with long distance lens as orgy with Japan Town drug
Czar   is in full swing   Tatiana?  *Niet*.  She is not there

# DOLLY

Hina style is maximum ancient, unique-
minuscule-tiny extra dainty and avec detail
exquisite. Vraiment. It is also meaningful
sacred spirit of cherry blossom most antique
orchard in Japan Town aristocrat clique
of which Lady Mamiko is regal
status, bien sur, it is now official
knowledge she is making maximum mystique
preparation far beyond Blossom Party
Deputy behaviours this season
for it may be the ultimate occasion
when Maman is strong against carcinoma-nasty
extremity with deep rotten
flesh emergency lifeline situation.

Emergency lifeline situation in Maine
did claim Maman's sister Andrée in minutes
that tick tocks slow as when Le Général fails to meet
deadline for Miss Ting awaiting steam-engine train
that is not arriving at Barbieville Station
when expected!  It is maximum absolute

joke abomination, vraiment, and best route
anyway to make corridor short-cut connection
by pantry and kitchen where our latest
housekeeper weeps of hellish distraught overworked
from preparations drudgeries domestic
and ridiculous ungrateful saying she is underpaid!
What constant nag-disaster, with all perks
this job did offer. Is it not for all of us hectic?!

Is it not extreme hectics for us all? Pah!
Dolly does not make jelly-shake fuss over trifle-
blancmange experiences extra trivial!
Le Général is understanding this urgency far
more easy than others. Such bravery! Each new hour
he is making long trek to Barbieville!
East or West Side he is super volunteer-helpful
to make la vie for Dolly simple in this regard.

Dolly is appointing him Chief-Deputy Cherry-
Operation Assistant Officer
as special benefit for extra friends to treat.
He is Tweety Pie yellow canary
darling this considerate service to make as offer
for Dolly's requirements beaucoup to meet.

To meet Dolly's requirements beaucoup
changes and particulars for every doll's need
is exhausting but for Maman-love she must lead
all dolls with extreme égalité attitude!
Exception: trash-trailer vinyls sans gratitude

most obvious as it is best fair agreed
they are not of suitable stylish or creed.
Exception: baby-chubbies avec hyacinth blue
eyes and autumn lips to envisage future
as séance medium soothsayer childs.

Dolly's humility is un grand fashion object
commes slogan T-Shirt diamante Dior!—
also smiley face badge pin or Live Aids
Lady Di–John Elton concert special charity project.

In memory for Andrée special charity
project is Girl Scouts which she makes to adore
when she is thunder-sky lovesick to mourn
after top secrets teenage love-crush is far behind enemy
frontier same way as Papa fought as cowboy
to quell Indian braves and Lakota warrior
Sioux-Apache from Texas to Oregon
while he is college student of mineral geology
specialist last century. Pouf! Andrée makes bird nest
hobby Kodak camera in wilderness
which Maman-Huguette helps develop
photographs avec Dolly who is to learn best
accomplishments as official allotted children's
companion of whom all dolls is deep jealous!

As special companion of whom all dolls is jealous
it is honourable to stand apart
from others who comprehend not this artifice
which is sometimes to make more precious

each individual relationship and not to spit vicious
slanders when it is happy sacrifice
for us dolls. Dolly would not think twice
if Andrée was alive, non, non, Dolly would make spacious
maximum capacity for both adorable sisters
as there is distinction avec genetic
connectivity function of all mannequin
loyalty and gilded swan behaviours.
There is such mode as elegant etiquette.
It is an inheritance most gladdening.

It is a most saddening inheritance.
Maman holds crystal paperweight on millions
and millions of dollars! Yet not any monnaies can enliven
this once intrepid sister Andrée whose intelligence
is by all who feel her appreciated at once!
Instead Huguette-Maman listens to choir-boy requiem
in Bronx New York Cemetery Woodlawn.
Dolly's most anxious pulse only alleviates since
exacts moment when black automobile cortege
is arrived a la maison for private
family only away from public eye-stares.
Most distraught is la petite fille Maman-Huguette
whose character of shyness is not suitable to emulate
or understand the death of a beloved flesh sister.

# MEXICAN BARBIE

Ancestors dictate   many things   like being   rich or flat
broke   In Mexico   we   keep   in touch     it's not exactly

Christian      you call it superstition!   We celebrate
*Dia de los muertos*  honouring  those  who walk with us

electric and invisible   Andrée was    like this,  her
faith in her little sister    Huguette   endlessly unshakeable

Ghosts can't die    dolls neither, but we do like to party
hard     This is our vocation & there's no better place than

*Isla de las Muñecas*    a magical   garden & shrine
just south of Mexico City:  lilies shimmy in canals

kids  can choose  between tantalising vision, a
lullaby or mariachi    marching! It is a starry   *memento*

*mori* to a little girl who also lost   sisters  & drowned in
nebulous currents   swirling like Don Julian,   drunk on

*octli* a fiery cactus water    too late  to  save her  though he
pulled her body out        & made it everafter    a lifelong

quest to populate  his island    *I want my dolly!* was her last
request  Hardly an Aztec sacrifice!   All it takes   is one

skeleton    to shake his maracas   or a blindfolded child to
thwack the piñata   at a birthday party  so hard it

unleashes us   Or else a kilo of blossom!  Wow!
Viva La Isla!  We shout and stamp our dainty feet &

whoosh   we arrive !    Every doll dreams of nights in
Xochimilco—We are   indestructible      friends

your unquestioning companions, less like dogs, more like
zombies:    we might tear off an arm     gnaw on a leg!

# DOLLY

**907 Fifth Avenue, Apartment 8W**
*26 March 1991 5.46 a.m.*

Dolly has been awakened from her late afternoon nap by the din from Barbieville. She sits up in her bed and rubs her eyes, then looks across to check on Maman. She is not there! Dolly leaps up and runs to the bathroom. It too is empty. She begins to rummage, lifts the coverlet, dives to the floor, looks under the bed. Where is Maman? Dolly pauses, picks up one of the Polaroids littering the floor.

—What is this ridiculous?—Dolly mumbles under her breath, before flinging the offending image aside and picking up another and peering at it with a look of vague recognition.

## BARBIEVILLE DISCOTHEQUE

A glitterball dangles from the ceiling, an array of desk lamps point up, scattering its rainbow-like Skittles across the chequered dancefloor. DJ Kenny Ken rollerskates underneath in green and white basketball shorts and vest, a Sony Walkman on his head. A black mixing desk constructed from two transistor radios turned on their side is garlanded by a Cartier charm bracelet, its ruby cupids and emerald-tailed lovebirds glinting in the corner to reveal a tangle of naked Barbies and Kens. Centre stage we see Malibu Barbie coiled around one of the silver poles that run the length between each shelf. Swiss Barbie is holding her long plait to one side as she leans across a booth, snorting a lurid pink powder through a helter-skelter straw.

Dolly blinks and tosses the photograph aside.

Christie Barbie sits cross-legged in a rattan chair, nodding her head and mouthing the chorus to Crystal Waters' 'Gypsy Woman', *la da di da de da, she's homeless*, while blowing smoke rings from a hookah pipe and waving a stick of nag champa. Dolly is slumped over a booth, a cocktail umbrella in her hair, her skirts & petticoats pulled up above her waist, revealing her jointed wooden legs. A Martini glass is toppled over.

In the bottom right-hand corner, something furry and blurry—There's no door to the adjacent, double-aspect living room, but a mouse, harnessed to a Sylvanian Families horse and cart loaded with confetti, scurries along the skirting board and disappears into an arched hole—

—These vinyl-faces are not caring for Dolly! It is abominations, when Maman is missing and we are facing deep devastations.— Non, non, non, non. Dolly is too much the martyr with these special photo projects! This is yesterday! We must be readying tomorrow & last nights! We must be avec les valises—she shakes her head, her four little teeth biting down onto her top lip, puts on a black eye mask, tucking the elastic behind her petite ears and lies back down on her bed, her thoughts swirling noisily as she goes over the events of the last few weeks in her head before eventually drifting into listless sleep.

When clouds skitter across bleak sky, a dark mood
descends, outside and within, swirls
of buffeting winds de change and flurries
of lightnings and thunder claps—we're headed

we don't know where. It is a choice most hard
and difficile to decide: must Dolly bring this girl
Adele or that boy Jules avec les yeux bleus and blond curls?
Bien sur, she is not yet certain, mais should

Maman make recovery avec lotion Cherry B
ointment-powder we are together for
eternity again which is for future ideals.

Meanwhile Dolly sends memo to each miniature figurine,
each doll and automaton to pack one carry-on size suitcase or
small trunk of necessities for their travel.

If it is necessary to travel, with a trunk
or valise even, Dolly is in trouble
to consider beaucoup outfits beautiful:
frilly collars, beaux chapeaux—mais also junk
stuffs! Lady Mamiko is best to help think
on this, her beauty is so minimal
in expression and now she makes double
activity avec Maman pour Hina Pink
Blossom Festival when petals must be gathered
delicate too for confettis and our top secret
project chemical so tough as tinpot knight helmet
which at les pieds of dog-leg balustrade stairs guards

over grandiose and stern portraits
of ancestors dressed in muffs and capes d'hermine.

Ancestors dressing in ermine capes and muffs
reside dans les maisons petites and grandes.
Maman's personal artist makes immortal chère Andrée
in gilt-frame painting and Dolly has one cuddle
cherub dans la chambre, his arms still chubby
and cushion-ish, his face soft gold by candle
fire when Dolly stares at dark space in her marbled
hearth thinking quietly of past things less ugly
and how Maman is long living for a flesh
creature mais now carcinoma-nasty smell
is strong like sirloin du boeuf in kitchen pantry.
Every week demands are made for cash
from prefecture departments as well as
commitments sentimental which are many.

Commitments sentimental are mainly
of eras and occasions historique
and Maman is generous beyond critique
in this style avoiding stranger charity
instead providing for child, cousin, aunty
long after our friend is expiring quite deceased.

Never did she construct our world as jeu d'esprit:
a doll is enlivened as is a pianoforte
and their notes struck true with love and practice,
playful aussi, as two twin boys in sailor suits
make mischief and bien sur extremes delight.

It is not sham façade or pure caprice
which makes us dolls a preference absolute.
We are here forever, through day and night.

Forever is not long through day or night
when Dolly is abandonné senses
similar mais deep apart from human existence.

This dream is illumined in different light:
it is a field of earth baked in the eye of white
sun, no poppy grows there only spiked fences
and houses avec corners and wall absences
no furnitures or paintings only a flight
of steps leading nowhere but to empty air
and doorways in light wood unpainted, my voice
splinters but there is no response, no echo,
angles are every place yet each escalier
he is begging for foot pressure in this void
where there is no doll, no human, no echo.

There is no doll, no human, no echo
as loud as this most uncivilised noise
machine boom-boom-bang! Quelque chose
is this? Dolly is awakened and can hear Le Disco
more clear than fresh vinegar makes window
panes squeaks! Les Vinyl-Faces are doing this Vogue
craze Madonna-Virgin dance in leather clothes
dans les pantalons avec holes-culots!
Apparently they are naming these garments 'chaps'
which is favourite of Dolly's best singer Freddy

Mercuries although only when Maman cannot hear
as for her Queen-music is dégueulasse
mais maintenant this is far from hardly
the point as Dolly is holding tight her ears.

As Dolly is holding her ears tight le point
is cette musique is only big difference avec Maman
and now DJ Kenny Ken spins les chansons
'white label' and Le Dancefloor is stomping en points
pour un chorus *she's homeless, she's homeless* . . . not once
but many times she must complain
as to healths and safetys situations mais Dolly refrains
from such incivility as matter of point
particular as next song is her favourite Vanilla Ice
extraordinary handsome
who Dolly has viewed on new channel MTV
after Lisette was those times turning off *Miami Vice*
rerun to transcribe for Maman more Flintstones
episodes lasting long as infinity.

Infinity is un episode long
and troubling to decipher, 'Dirty Cash' is better
as is 'I Touch Myself' video pour
Divinyls pop-star group who sing hit song
one wonder to forget troubles which are too strong
and eloquent as red-satin Dalí sofa
lips positioned by leopard-skin wallpaper.
We dolls have done no criminal wrong.

It is Mardi in March, vingt-six, after

noons o'clock.  The telephone rings, loud. Importantly.
Not this time of finance but insteads health.
It is finally a hospitals docteur.
He is wishing to examine carcinoma-nasty.
It is clear cut medical drama, life or death.

Clear-cut death or life medical drama
is how it looks on this day of judgement
seen on tarot card The Tower, seulement
this prophecy shows how Dolly's trauma
is justified fearful extravaganza
depicted by twenty two flammes and ten stems
from the tree of life which is old system
of knowledge ancient as Yokohama.

Maman must take treatment extra:
Cherry Blossom Powder is not enough goodness!
She is thin like concentration victim.

These facts are long time indisputable.
There is cavity ulcer instead of eyehoods.
We must ask Miss Ting again for her prediction.

# ASTRONAUT BARBIE

Apollo 11! 10-9- The future's now!  We wedged our flag
between        two intergalactic  rocks round as Dolly's  butt

cheeks!      It's hard—dealing with all that perspective
Down on the ground is a mess!    A spinster with an

Electra complex  Psychoanalysis 101  Maman's frigid as a
freeze-dried strawberry, petrified of old age, but who fears

gravity    when your breasts are    moulded plastic?  A
hypochondriac hermit, it's ironic how she ended up

incapacitated    & sick as a dog    as if that itsy bitsy
journey to the foyer on a stretcher  was hard as climbing

K2, or a mission to Mars! She was trembling like poor
little Laika    that cute pup   the Ruskies sent up to the

moon all alone, to orbit the Earth   Maman clung to her
nursey  like a cliff edge    crumbling   in her hands

Outer space is a time warp  but in the apartment those
porcelain  dollies can't take the pressure, they literally crack

Quantum mechanics could maybe turn back the clock
RIP: no one wants that    monogrammed on their

scratch-resistant visor.  Why starve to death? Hun, get a
tummy tuck!   You got more dollars than rice in China

Up here your problems look like   a speck of dirt on
Venus!  Do I have to beam you down an MRI by satellite?

Walking on the moon's better than space dust from Planet
X they didn't even discover yet and as for Cherry? That's

yesterday's news  Let Dolly and the General live in the past! I gotta
zoom!    I've a degree in astrophysics & an asteroid to orbit

# MISS TING

**907 Fifth Avenue, Apartment 8W**
*26 March 1991 8.17 a.m.*

Miss Ting Say

Dolly come push up 'erself wit 'er airs an' graces, but is me, Miss Ting, My General look pon out dicorner of 'im one eye. Is me, Miss Ting, mek im forget bout Malibu Barbie an' er long leg, orange as ortanique, that flex up n round the backside a her 'ead, thigh-top press h'against 'er earhole so.

Miss Ting Say

Dolly think she so-so special, servin' Dar-Jeelin tea, from high peak inna India from 'er Chinee cup n saucer. Yes, mi darlin' me did see how yuh can look tru it like cloudy water when yuh hold it up to di sky. Yes, mi did tek care when I wash it up and place it pon drainin' board, jus so! Ya no know se General G nuah prefer fi drink Guinness punch or sarsaparilla pon verandah with me, Miss Ting? No suh! Him nuah care two owl hoot fi Lady Muck Lah-di-Dah Mi Ah Come From Forrin Dress in Stiff White Crinoline Finery.

Is me, Miss Ting

 does know how fi keep real company. An' is Miss Ting tight poonani 'im slide inna afta im tongue mek it slippry an' wet. A Miss Ting bed 'im roll out of Sunday marnin before 'im straighten 'im dicky bow necktie an' sneak into mahogany pew beside 'er inna chapel. Let 'im hand brush lightly pon 'er knee. Don't think me nuah catch dat. Is Miss Ting know how fi siddown pon it, how fi lick 'im head like lollipop. Is me, Miss T, mek 'im werk up sweat, wring saltwater rivulet from the back of 'im neck, an' run down the gully a him backbone. Is Miss Ting ah go pump seed from 'im hard bamboo. An Lah-di-Dah-Dolly think she can snatch my man's white meringue with 'er pale face an' lace an' French macaroon?

And now, is me, Miss Ting

 Dolly run to fi tea-leaf reading cos she cyaan find Lady Mamiko fi fling down I-Ching an' tell 'er how fi fix-up er precious Maman whose mout' spout like Dunns River Fall every time she drink 'er coffee inna de mornin'. And no, Miss Ting nah 'tink 'erself lucky' to be up on top floor o' h'uptown apartment lookin' out at Central Park lake with heron an' rowboat tru dutty glass. Now Maman's face go hollow deeper than Potoo Hole ah Jackson Bay, dem Irish maids is long gone and di window dem not clean pon di hinside or out. Back home Miss Ting did look out pon ocean more blue than lapis stone. More sparkling than any fancy Jumeau doll glassy eye.

And now Lady Lah-di-Dah-Dolly comes beggin' me, Miss Ting,

 a fine rag doll wit pert soft titty, not dat unnatural badda-bing-silicone-look-ting on di Barbie dem, beggin' me to come catch grounds to swirl in er minuscule Wedgwood cup and saucer. Tea leaf too. Lady Mamiko flittin' bout like a hummingbird sip-sipping from this n that hibiscus flower, gettin' all her teeny tiny Japan-dolly done up nice for dem special party wit pretty-pretty red paper lantern an' sake wine refreshment. So is me, Miss Ting, Dolly wan fi spread purple cloth pon table, draw cards now Lady Mamiko too busy fi Dolly drama h'evry wakin' minute.

So Miss Ting, mi did tell Dolly straight

*Mi nah work no obeah, Miss Ting nah h'operate so! Is palm mi ah read an' dream. Tea leaf, coffee ground.* Is a natural ting. Ital mystic. And anyway, me ask 'er, *You nah cure this carcinoma-nasty already with yuh pink powder?*

Of course, Miss Ting know it nah make no difference and not likely to neither. Doll is doll an' flesh is flesh. Scientist Barbie an' 'er laboratory crew busy enuff with Sweet Cherry Factory true true. It h'operate all night so it seem but she nah mek no progress to crack di formula. An' General G down there so every five minutes on errand dis, favour dat, telling me is critical situation 'im a deal wit. Raasclaat.

If Miss Ting spread out 'er purple cloth

she go mek Dolly wait, same way Dolly take 'er time and mek um and ah about which doll she go select if push come to shove. Shove and push already happen, nuff a dem dolly go queue up and jostle Friday night to volunteer fi guinea pig duty to test the high-grade Cherry. Choa. Miss Ting nah go grovel pon hand and knee fi fun nor fashion. No sir. Everyting I need go come to me.

# CHINESE BARBIE

Asia is a continent, much much
        bigger than Japan Town—in

China we are the Masters of
        dim sum & far far larger

economies of scale. Dolly's
        fortune cookie advised her to

*Give it up* just as the Brits had to with
        Hong Kong. I don't think

isolation is so splendid, maybe a
        jade necklace will bring luck or a

Kung Fu General with some
        leadership skills. Her problem's

manufacturing, not distribution.
        *Ni hao!* It's 1991 & we're in the Year

of the Sheep or the Goat? Take your
> pick, but I know what I'd do, her

*qi* is depleted & sluggish, she
> really needs to up her game plan.

Sino-Franco relations could take a
> turn for better or worse, prices go

up & they go down. If she wants
> value for money then she might

want to think twice, I can guarantee
> exponential growth & a superior

Yin-Yang situation plus I'll throw a
> zodiac reading into the bargain.

# THE GENERAL

*Reminiscences & Recollections of General Obadiah
Louverture Little Rock Yellow Bird Junior the Second*

## A MEMOIR

General Obadiah Louverture Little Rock Yellow Bird Junior the
Second. That is my full, unabridged & Endowed Name. & It is
a hitherto undisclosed fact that the 'General' as referred to is not
George Armstrong Custer, the gonorrhoea-ridden Union Army
Officer with whom Eliza found her life entwined, but another,
more appropriate warrior.

Toussaint Louverture: General, Jacobin-Noir & Revolutionary
extraordinaire, who had led the Incarcerated of Haiti into that
historic & victorious rebellion all those centuries ago. He, who
liberated our Land of the High-Priestess-Mannequin-Clan, where
the Veil between Soft-Flesh & Doll-Hive was worn thin as any
hand-me-down Sunday Best. Where a Fat moon blazed its path
through tavern windows in flickering candlelight as marauding
Pirates & press-ganged Sailors swigged draughts by the dozen,
Blind to the true identities of the grinning Revolutionaries &
Buxom Maroons who surrounded them on stealthy reconnaissance

so as to gather muskets & coordinates through the intoxicated waggling of ale & rum-loosened Tongues. This was a lush & prolific island where legions of Martyr-Mannequins sacrificed Arms, Legs, Lungs & Necks as cushions for carefully placed pins to help bring a nation of whip-wielders to its Knees.

Grandmammie Bessie stitched this history into my striped britches & matching DickyBow from a worn Waistcoat she'd wheedled out of old Miser Pryce. Gollywog? I think not, my Friend, for it is I, General Obadiah Louverture Little Rock Yellow Bird Junior the Second who was the prototype. Those mawkish minstrels were a facsimile of me! Of every Black Flesh fashioned Rag-Mannequin. It was Grandmammie Bessie herself who collected used cloth, rags & Horse-Hair from the Manes & Tails of prized Palominos with which to stuff me; she who haggled hard for those two, matching, Ivory buttons at the haberdashery – as the top-right corner of the back section in the general store was somewhat grandiosely titled – *A little piece of Africa* she'd muttered under her Breath, as the needle pierced her Fingertip for Blood that dripped upon the cloth & she fastened tight the thread.

*

& So, we find Eliza Brown in the big house kitchen, not squeezing frothy, yellow-tinted Milk from ruminating Cows in the dank, straw-strewn shed with Hannah & Bessie, who at fifty was tired yet still strong of Heart, Liver & Mind & anyway had the skills already her granddaughter was yet to learn. Old Miser Robert had become infirm & a Nursemaid was required to empty the Blood & tar-muddled Phlegm that filled the Spitoon by his creaky iron bed, examine his Blood-streaked Stools, change & launder his soiled sheets & prepare a thin yet restorative broth that his malfunctioning Bowels & Belly could endure. There was also the job of Listening to a 'Treasure-Chest' of Scatter-Brained reminiscences with an air that announced interest rather than irritation. Even more challenging a task was that of keeping the pendulum of Mistress Pryce's voracious Ego content, as it swung between vulnerable & vindictive with a speed & bustle that only Eliza's youth & inexperience could adequately counter.

As was her way, Eliza decided this dubious honour had been bestowed upon her for reasons of individual merit & Hannah let that illusion flower. A young Girl with thwarted horizons should have a chance to aspire. Additional to these Motherly ministrations, was the knowledge that Old Pryce was now too poorly for his Hands to follow where his Gaze had always alighted.

& That the damage had already been done. Also additional, was the reassurance that learning to cook for White-Flesh could only be advantageous: knowing how to conjure something tasty for the inhabitants of The Cabin was a necessary & common accomplishment. It was a prized & lesser-known fact that to take control of that most susceptible & voracious of Organs, the Stomach, could effect a degree of power & autonomy that only prowess over embers, cleaver, Carcass & cauldron could exact.

That Hannah had carefully & consistently tended to Old Pryce's Tumor over many, painstakingly observed seasons, with a watchful attention that knew when to aggravate & when to allay, was a skill not only of culinary, but military precision. Revenge for the brutal Iniquities of the Son & his rapacious Friends, as meted out to her Slender-Hipped & barely Menstruating daughter, was finally to be eaten, tepid as a Turd, by the Father – for anything more direct would have been vulnerable to detection.

*Wait* she had hissed to an incandescent Obadiah when the source of Eliza's thunderous moods & swollen Womb came to light. Hannah herself had waited as long as she might to tell Obadiah, afraid rage would overcome his survival instinct; that Eliza had not been sold from under them was a Godsend & one which any act of rebellion or blame could jeopardise.

& So, Hannah who was meticulous in terms of the quantity & quality of the moon-ripened herbs & 'spices' she scattered into her keepers' victuals, stepped up her campaign as she instructed her Headstrong Daughter on how to procure & distribute her 'remedies' through tasty stew & soup. The Old Coot sipped the broth Eliza spooned into his slack & dribbling Mouth as if his life depended on it, which, Hannah wryly noted, it did. The true properties of the concoction she would reveal to her obdurate off-spring in time. For the remonstrations as to Baby John's naming still stung & moreover, the whole episode had made it glaringly apparent that Eliza would have to feel what could not be taught. Deference, whether dictated or deserved, did not come easily to all.

\*

Huguette Clark collected dolls; George Armstrong Custer collected dogs. & Women. There was Mollie, Fanny, Nettie, Eliza, Libbie, Monasetah. More of these Soft-Flesh females in due course. In Dakota Territory his semi-feral pack numbered forty. Those estimates were trivial. Custer had Deerhounds & Bloodhounds, a Racoon Hound Pup. There were black Dogs, brown Dogs, pure breeds & mongrels. Lurchers & Layabouts. Snifters & Snouts. There was Tusk – a Catahoula Leopard Dog – a noble pooch of the Choctaw people & champion of the hunt:

no Raccoon or Possum or Fox could escape the dreaded clamp of his Bone-crushing Mandibles. Then there was Ginnie, a pungent house Pet, which is the official if not accurate term – who slept, curled like a Catherine Wheel on a Wolf-Skin rug, her nervous, snappity nature dormant but ready to erupt. Then there was his dearly beloved piebald – Rose, named after & often mistaken for Lady-Flesh, such was the gush of adoration whenever she came up in the General's florid correspondence.

Additional, there was a considerable number of desperate, worm-infested, mange-ridden Mutts who paddled across the swirling currents of the Potomac in order to keep up with the rest of the General's entourage; mongrel Bitches with Pups at the Nipple who crept out from the Underbelly of covered wagons where they hid from the blaze of afternoon sun to Tongue-Loll faithfully at the Toe-Tips of their Master's Boots.

Above all, was the bellicose & utterly indulged Lord Byron, an English Greyhound from Detroit; a Lip-Curling, precocious, Jack-Rabbit-chomping reprobate who liked nothing better than to stick his twitchy, aristocratic Nose deep into the crack of his odious & odorous Anus & snuffle therein as if he were rooting out the finest Périgord truffles. Or he was holding his ground, farting deep into the Horse-Hair mattress & licking his pink & slightly Furry Balls, pointedly, as Custer's Doggedly possessive & oft cuckolded Wife attempted to oust the succubus Cur from the marital bed with a broom – an aggression Byron resisted with an entitlement so absolute it was worthy to compete with that of his Master, whose multiple acts of genocidal savagery were uniformly applauded by the delusionary Settler-Flesh masses.

What, you might well ask, did this pack of Tick-snuffling, Flea-bitten, gas-emitting, vagabond Quadrupeds have to do with me,

General, Obadiah, Louverture, Little Rock, Yellow Bird? It is an astute question & it brings us back to the fortunes & adventures of the plucky Eliza. For it was she who gathered her few belongings in August 1863 on hearing that a makeshift Contraband Camp was gathering at the tents of the Seventh Cavalry Division. Contraband! What better word could describe the uniquely proprietorial Mindset under which Flesh traded Flesh, even at that time of mass rebellion & flight. That she ended up on the payroll & under the patronage of a White-Flesh General was opportune, even if his reputation for virtue & valour was as mythical as Medusa's writhing, Serpentine Hair. Admittedly, he rode, Cock-a-Whoop into battle on many occasion, fancying & fashioning himself on the very Chiefs he sought to annihilate: his covetous aims hidden even from his own consciousness in the bid to destroy that which his Heart secretly desired.

& Now it is of this charlatan that I write. A young officer, by definition a Yank, who cared not a jot for Emancipation although his geographic alignment positioned him North not South. I hear now with my invisible Ears a sharp intake of Breath. For did he not, as his Bulldog-Terrier-White-Flesh-Wife wrote in her self-serving memoirs, insist on Eliza sitting together with them at table in the dining car as they travelled cross country in that First Class railroad car? A transportation wrung from the Sweat & Sinew of Black-Flesh & Yellow-Skin gangs at the expense of the Red, whose lands & livelihoods evaporated with the great Plumes of steam from the engine's chimney. Did this supposedly chivalrous intervention, refusing the petulant & entitled demands of an officious & of course, lowly railway car manager, not underline the sincerity of his evocation for Equality?

Balderdash! Did Custer not bring Eliza back a Bison-Skin

blanket as a trophy from the Massacre the White-Flesh called a Battle at Washita? A slaughter he Cock-a-Doodle-Crowed, his Chest puffed & his Feathers a-bristle with the Adrenaline of pillage. Do not succumb to this Chevalier fakery, I beg you! For it was nothing more than his customary *My Cook! My wife & I, because I am Custer & I am a General with A Cook! My Dogs, My brothers, My military men – all shall do My Will in this new world, which I shall take by acre & by inch! Rifles cocked, ready to pick off a hundred Head of Shaggy-Bearded Bison from the vast, Thunder-Hooved Herds?*

& so it is August. Eighteen Hundred & Sixty Three. Two weeks in & the ground is dry & hard underneath Eliza's Feet, Feet that felt the pressure of every stone through the worn & thinning Soles of her hand-me-down Boots. Feet that, unlike those of her 'mistress' – a nomenclature these key-jangling jailors in such times insisted upon – were nearly as wide as they were long. Feet that were used to trudging uneven terrain, from the big house to the village & back, hurrying on this errand & that, whether rain fell or sun burned.

Eliza was young & quick & any missive on which she was sent was always doubly Capitalised. Hannah had taught her Daughter to scan the roadside with a Hawk's Eye: herbs & roots & seasonal fruit were gathered in basket & apron. Wild lettuce, chicory, bramble blackberries & blueberries, sorrel & dandelion leaves & roots, pawpaws, plums & persimmons. No natural provision went unforaged; no sage bush unremarked or located; no nettle tip unpicked. These skills would stand Eliza in good stead: for it was her inherited ability to make something tasty out of the thinnest air.

Thin air was all that stood between a lifetime of unpaid domestic drudgery coupled with the ever-impending threat of sexual attack & actual sexual attack & the possibilities of freedom & advancement in the Camp.

Thin air & the inquisitive Eyes of Baby-John, who was Toddle-Flesh now. Twenty-four moons & always dashing here & there—Mindless of any physical obstacle that stood in his way. Too heavy these months for Eliza to strap to her Back in a cotton papoose. Better to leave him home at the farm, for he was long-weaned yet emotionally tethered to the warm & capacious Bosom of Grandmammie Bessie, whose firm Hands he yielded to when she set him between her Knees on the kitchen stoop to pick Lice eggs from his Scalp & oil & plait his Hair. Best leave him to play peek-a-boo under the tattered flap of Hannah's dusty apron than to drag him through ditch & bramble patch to face *God only knows what kind of mud-caked, whisky-soaked squalor* at Amisville.

Better the devil they knew in the guise of Tom Bradbury, attentive neighbour, family friend & unrepentant rapist, who had volunteered, readily, to *keep an Eye on things*. Things, in this case, being *his* progeny John, *his* unwilling teenage concubine Eliza – who had become adept at never walking out to the river, the woods or the village alone & now, Hannah feared, the barely pubescent Marie-Louise, Isaac's younger sister who was not long twelve. Better to keep little John close, than have him snatched from her daughter's Arms, to be sold on at auction to an entrusted (oftentimes Brown-Flesh) overseer from a cotton plantation in Alabama the size of a small town never to be seen, scolded or Cuddled again. If Eliza was determined to *try her luck*, which she undoubtedly was, she'd have a better chance without mother and grandmother to slow the young'uns down. Hannah told her daughter in no uncertain terms, she could fetch the littl'un once the Yankees won the war & she'd achieved all she'd set her Sights upon. Whichever the sooner or the later.

Many smallholdings in Western Virginia were now abandoned, as White-Flesh families retreated south to safety as the Union cavalry advanced, scooping up Runaways & Quadruped-Chattel along the way. Despite, or perhaps because of his infirmity, and with their Son at War & posted *the good Lord Jesus only knew where*, Old Miser & Mistress Pryce had quit the smallholding as soon as their high-bridged Caucasian Noses caught wind of Custer's camp, which was barely three miles up the road & round the corner. Perhaps what alerted the elderly couple to the imminent encroachment of hostile Union forces was the whiff of raw onions on the breeze, the General's favourite; maybe it was the noisy & reactive chain of barks & howls Custer's stinky pack & rag-taggle band of military misfits, critters & profiteers inevitably set off in any new vicinity.

Either way, on that already warm, August dawn, Eliza quietly ushered Isaac and Marie-Louise through the gate & latched it behind them, more from habit than necessity. That she stuffed me Headfirst into her bulging knapsack was a surprise. It did not occur to me that the grieving Mother would dislodge me from under the crook of her sleeping Son's Arm, a crystalline Tear landing dead centre above my third Eye, which at this hour was wide open as I joined Baby John in a Thumb-sucking dream of succulent corn cobs consumed upon Grandmammie Bessie's toasty Lap.

Truth be enunciated I sometimes forgot that Eliza was so distressed. Over the years she had learnt to conceal her feelings judiciously, lest they be discovered & exploited by any number of predatory individuals, who were prone to protecting what they considered to be any infringement of their 'interests' with varying degrees of ferocity, whether subtle or overt. I had become complacent as my focus was of course Baby John. It wasn't until she raised my Tummy & its snip-snappy braces to her Nose & Lips &

inhaled deeply, that I realised what surrogate I was! Or, indeed, that Baby John's acrid, Urine-tainted aroma that only a Mother might adore, was a scent I carried.

As it happened, that scent had utility, although not for us, the runaways. For it took less time than expected for Tom Bradbury's Hairy Nostrils to twitch & flare, first in suspicion & then in outrage before setting his Hounds upon us. That these Canines were old, overfed & underwhelmed was divine intervention, for their enthusiasms lay more in the immediate potential of recently occupied Rabbit holes where snoozing Bunny-Kits might be snuffled & crunched.

Had this been but a year previous, Eliza's Heart might have leapt from her Chest in fear for life & Limb. & Indeed danger was all about. In America, South or North, the principle of property & ownership was as sacred to White-Flesh as the Bison was to the Cheyenne or Lakota. Virginia was a border state & even though the Yankees were advancing the Rebels had their chains & manacles ready and rattling for any Runaway Black-Flesh whether they were Free or Fettered. Each carried a price on Head, Hands, Feet, Belly & Back, Pussy & Prick & that 'property' was protected, vigorously, by an unceasing & precise violence that was designed to discourage & deter. The whip was applied to split & sting, to break the Spirit, not the Spine; for permanent physical damage had a detrimental effect on economics. *A slave in the grave was a dollar in the ditch*, as Old Miser Pryce liked to mutter & all rates of attrition were carefully weighed & considered.

On this occasion, Eliza's bid for freedom was urged on by Hermes himself, for her flight from the farm was aided by the fact that the Union troops at Amissville had virtually camped on *their* doorstep & were a mere three miles away.

Old Miser & Mrs Pryce had departed South hurriedly, leaving the Cabin inhabitants in charge of the modest tract of farmland – Land they already tilled, toiled in and managed for all intents & purpose – along with a few candlesticks, a tarnished silver tea pot, Milk jug, sugar bowl, chiming clock & various other cumbersome paraphernalia that was neither portable not sentimental enough to take with them. Eliza helped Obadiah bury these 'treasures' under the shadow of an old oak at the top of the far field. That she had decided to leave the safety of the Cabin to take her chances on the open road, where any local Busybody might fling her to a gang of ragged & increasingly feral Confederates – or take matters into their own, Bloodthirsty Hands – says much about that wretched & barbarous institution, however benign & charitable its perpetrators claimed to be.

& So it was, that Eliza & Isaac, little Marie-Louise & I, General Obadiah, Louverture, Little Rock, Yellow Bird Junior the Second pitched up at the camp, she slightly out of Breath from both exertion & excitement, my Neck bent to a crick amongst a cram of earthy roots gathered along the way. Sweat ran down her Nape & Forehead & clustering along the contours of her upper Lip & she wiped it away lest it betray a scent of fear intermingled with ferocious anticipation. There were all kinds of Men, in & out of uniform, Muscled & gaunt, rugged & war-torn, Weasel-Eyed & more than occasionally handsome, such was the pallor of their youth. They gathered around tents & makeshift cabins: runaways & Free-Flesh sat alongside Pink-Faced boys, juvenile enough for Pimples, yet old enough to carry a rifle or revolver, pull its trigger & kill a Man. Slinking between Shin & Ankles, Noses a-twitch, Gums spotted pink & black & slobbering, were Custer's private army of Pooches, who would patrol the compound in search of scraps, pausing unannounced to Cock a Leg, or crouch, shudder & Shit.

From my upturned vantage point I saw the crowd bristle with anticipation – for these mangy Curs announced their Lord & Master as out & abroad & making his daily inspection! From my slightly elevated position, my Face squashed, my left Eye peeping through a small tear in the cloth, I was able to discern the lanky Frame & strutting gait of the Yankee Boy Wonder as he approached the huddle of Black Flesh folks, whom Eliza & her companions had gravitated towards. Custer cast his Buzzard Eyes over her teenage Flesh, from the slant of her dark Neck down to her high & slender Waist & firm Behind. I witnessed those Eyes as they travelled & wandered, through every cavern & imagined valley; I saw that glint & flicker of lust & scheme. For Custer liked nothing better with a Woman, or indeed a Hound, than a challenge.

That Eliza was flattered by Custer's attention would have been obvious only to those that knew her well. For those who didn't, the Dark-Flesh-Matron, with wooden spoons & cleaver stuffed in apron pocket & a feisty, fearsome demeanour was the vision they (& she) were most ready to believe in. Yet to me it was a physical fact, heightened by her instinctive response, which had been to reposition the bag I occupied & clutch it, tight, to her Solar Plexus. Truth is many of those assembled were Boys, not Men, & it was this reconfiguration of her material presence, as Matriarch & Mama to all, that became her means of mortal survival in a camp ruled by bravado, Testosterone & the Adrenaline required to counter the thrill & exhaustion of combat, killing & denial.

The General's gaze was swift, almost perfunctory, but it lingered in all the obvious places long enough. Eliza knew That Look. Ye there was something in Custer's swagger. A certain allure in the almost Child-Like curl of his orange Hair, the droop & twitch of his stew- & mud-flecked Moustache, the jaunt with which he rearranged his broad-brimmed black hat. It was a sensation that surprised & repulsed her in equal measure. For up to this point, Eliza's only intimate experience had been far from voluntary.

Catching the Eye of a General was a different matter, for a Man of Power & Influence may well have what she truly desired: paid work. From inside the knapsack, my Ear-Space pressed hard against Eliza's sturdy Spine, I could hear the rush of Blood pumping through her Veins, a smothered rasp of Breath rise & fall through the back of her Ribcage, while my Doll-Eye did discern the Electricity-tingle from Nipple to Clitoris, a ripple of repulsion & attraction intermingled, that her conscious Mind bid her hastily to dismiss.

Custer stood not a Foot away, his Hand propping up his Chin, in a theatrical affectation of conjecture, as if he were Rodin's beloved Thinker, or the Greek, Aristotle. With his boot-heels & hat accounted for, the General was endowed with a rakish stature that enabled him to make physical advances that would have been noticed sooner in broader Men – & thus he positioned himself accordingly, standing so close, Eliza could smell a trace of jerky, coffee, cinnamon pomade & those raw onions he so loved on his Breath.

It was as much as she could muster not to wrinkle her Nose in distaste, for the intermingled scents were overpowering & one glimmer of repugnance – even construed as disinterest – would have been fatal. If not literally, then certainly professionally. In fact, it was the surreptitious stink of poorly attended, some- what festering venereal disease, wafting up from his overactive, undiscerning & leaky Penis that Eliza's alert olfactory Organ did detect, if unknowingly. That & the onions – for although the General was known to carry in his top pocket a Toothbrush at the ready to keep his Smile brightly charming, it did not mask the malodorous funk that swirled about him & his motley pack of Mutts. It was, in fact, the stench of those onions that saved her – for it was that same aroma that swirled about her memory of Tom Bradbury's first attack – & which made her know, incontrovertibly, that Custer was to be kept, always, at Arm's, Leg's & ideally Breath's length.

*I'm a cook, Sir*, she'd said – surprising herself in the certainty of her articulation, taking a small, surreptitious step back (yet maintaining a visual contact that was almost, but not quite, direct) – *a damn good cook who knows how to dodge a bullet while she peels, slices & sizzles an onion!*

# BALLERINA BARBIE

Arabesque!   Plié!  It is pleasure  & pain, to know
ballet!   I keep my hair in a tight high bun,   a silver

crown, tilted back on my head, atop a slender neck
Dancing's a brutal game  the body pays the price

Eat Nothing!  Maman   must do better   Discipline
Fortitude   Strong as the arch in my  foot   en pointe

Grace is always  contingent on timing.   No
heffalump twirled on a lake of tears   or survived thin

ice    There are many ways to enter or exit  a stage
Judgement    gets blurry  over the years  Everything you

know now   your gut knew then, truth stretches like a
leotard   The doctor says   old age, wear and tear

Maman is mortal    On earth to learn   Anorexia
Nervosa?     A feeding tube makes these things

obvious    Bulimia's more of a secret hobby
Pirouette!    This move   churns the stomach so it

quickens & spins like a  music box          automaton
Rhythm, routine    A patient's always at the mercy of

somebody's schedule   A metronome of dosage &
tomorrow,  so reminiscent of today, as a chorus is

uniform and tiresome    Distraction's a
valuable commodity, money drip drips and the

wealthy spend with    delirious abandon! You don't need
X-ray vision  to spot      a fracture   in the soul

Youth takes its toll  The spirit always reaches    for its
zenith  Finds comfort in strange, inexplicable  places

# LADY MAMIKO

In real life
Genji and The Empress are
quite indifferent.

> Any attraction
> fizzled out the thousandth time
> Maman made them kiss.

> > The Emperor tends
> > to get confused and grumpy
> > with his concubines.

> > The Empress
> > gets green-eyed jealous, which is
> > quite hilarious.

Now Genji pretends
to have brotherly feelings
towards The Princess.

I would love to walk amongst cherry blossom in Kyoto, in Nara, in Osaka. To feel a cool breeze, to inhale the intoxicating air. Japan Town's reproduction of Ryoan-Ji's rock garden is accurate in terms of measurement. But *sukura* is enthralling in an altogether different way.  It is beautiful to decide to be a tree. It is beautiful to be a tree. I see trees only from above. How I long to sit on a root, with a bento picnic lunch.

> Obviously
> Maman still feels like a ten
> thousand year-old girl.

This Matsuyama Castle project is ambitious and I have lost enthusiasm. I don't like having to hurry my Lady of the Bonsai, she likes to take her time.

> Hikaru likes men
> to fall to their knees: worship
> is really his thing.

> As if a brother
> should woo a sister even
> when she comes of age.

As I said, in the book they're not actually related, but the Princess is a child. Maman seems oblivious to the incestuous undertones. Sometimes her innocence is breathtaking.

Maman's only friend
Madame P says she will call
an ambulance soon.

Madame Pierre is the widow of Maman's old physician. When you are very rich and very old you tend to outlive your doctors. It is a testament to their professionalism I suppose. It's hardly convenient for a recluse though. New doctors must be acclimatised.

Violet light screams
from the television room
along the hallway.

As yesterday
Maman sends her food away—
Few birds are thinner.

Dolly has been fruffing and puffing all morning, about what to wear for the ceremony, who will go to the hospital, how she will select from the porcelains. It's a shame the ceremony clashes, but our celebrations are lunar. When the moon swells so will the Blossom.

My Lady beckons
from deep within the courtyard
shadows, eyes ablaze.

Her neck is a swan.
Her breast plump, so feathery!
She is my pillow.

A fan can conceal
and a fan expresses all
in precise fingers.

A long corridor
is a surreptitious place—
its walls glistening.

The General is quite furtive these days. He usually stops by to slurp some ramen and catch up on the news. Maman's dragged me all the way to her bedroom because she is making sketches of my kimono to send to Dior. I am sat atop her dresser and she has drawn the curtain for additional light. The room has definitely become more dusty and the copies of *Paris Match* and *The New Yorker* are stacking up now Lisette is no longer with us. She used to take them home for her daughter once Maman had finished with them. At least we will have rehearsal soon so I can return to my Lady. I had also arranged to meet The Scholar to practise calligraphy. The Porcelains seem edgy. It's hard not to feel sorry for them. They are so ill equipped for the modern world. I can't see them managing in the harsh light of a hospital ward.

The little frillies
are all seated on hall chairs,
bags on dimpled knees.

Glassy eyes open
wide and flickering with dreams
of swirling wind, leaves.

# ROYAL BARBIE FROM ENGLAND

Americans adore the Royal Family!
Big Ben, Buck House: paid by the

Civil List, that's taxpayers not the
Duke of York. The Chancellor of the

Exchequer handles it all, once a
fortnight I have to check my diary, the

Garden Party's always something of a
highlight, at Her Majesty's Pleasure!

In-joke, sorry. The days of medieval
jousting are over, apart from tithes cos

King Henry made a state of the church.
Legally I don't know the details but

Marie-Antoinette is a case in point.
Now this is the best bit—because

once Dolly gets By Royal Anointment
printed on her product she'll be

quintessentially untouchable, the dosh'll
roll in, anybody pisses her off

Scotland Yard looks straight into it.
That's how it works! You don't have to

understand anything, maybe pretend
Victorian values are up your Champs-Élysées.

Windsor Castle's lovely at Easter, no
expense spared on the refurb they did last

year, next Christmas we're going to Kenya or
Zanzibar on safari, tax-free charity work.

# THE GENERAL

*Reminiscences & Recollections of General Obadiah Louverture Little Rock Yellow Bird Junior the Second*

**A MEMOIR**

AnyBody can make history, only a great Man can write it. Oscar Wilde said this & a great many, wittier things, that Junior was fond of quoting. This Rag-Mannequin Scribe makes no claim to greatness, but write it I must. Rewrite it. That abominable cigar-puffing Bulldog the Brits do so adore, certainly made history & was accurate to his own endeavours no doubt when he said history was a pack of lies agreed upon. Our own Abraham Lincoln, another Soft-Flesh Trickster & who of course was President at this very time declared history truth & truth Etc, Etc. A doll's life, like a tree's, can be long, our memories tendrilous roots reaching into clammy Crevices—But it is that pack of lies, dressed as Dandy in silk finery, which Spurs this Wordsmith, that pushes pen to paper. For us dolls are intimates, confidantes of the Heartbeat, we know the flutter of Eyelash in dreamsleep, we Hear the truths from which Consciousness flinches.

Suffice to say, thusforth, my life on leaving the Cabin with Eliza, despite the absence of my Flesh-Child companion Baby John, and Grandmammie Bessie, my Creator, was improved; not through physical comfort, which as documented was Mutt-ridden to the last, but through the foul & fair winds & freedoms of the road. War, yes War, was among us, & the battlefields were Bloody & putrid. But, so too was Freedom & the wind that might ruffle one's Hair. Camping with the Yankees, with all its threats & deprivations, felt to a teenage Eliza, like she had landed in the right place at the right time & she was sure as hell gonna make the most of it. Eliza had pluck! & a Dogged determination that Cloaked her from danger, a protector more omniscient than the shield of Achilles.

& Thus we passed another five years together. Eliza dodging bullets & shrapnel & the General's lustful attentions, often finding the former less dangerous than the latter.  It was certainly a relief, albeit brief, when his fresh-Faced-Flesh-Bride arrived & Eliza no longer had to juggle ardour with appetite, unless of course it was a flirtation *she* decided she would cook up & take a Bite of. She also liked having her own kitchen & being in charge of it. The men nicknamed her The Queen of Sheba, for she wielded her hard-won & highly circumscribed power as skilfully as her spatula & skillet. She was the one who dished out favours, who knew how to manipulate & curry favour, alongside Deer & Rabbit & Squirrel when there was no Oxtail to make the General's favourite soup, for he too, like most of the Soft-Flesh-Males at the camp, & in the World as far as Eliza could discern, was more pliable when watered & fed & the Itch in his Loins was Scratched.

In the absence of Baby John she fed & watered Stray & Waif: one little Soft-Flesh, thin & reedy as a poor little picked Sparrow, even with its Nose running & its Thumb sucked, might wheedle its way under her Apron, was allowed on occasion to hang about &

Snuggle up around the campfire. At one moment I was perilously close to being gifted to a litlun she had a soft Spot for, a Boy, it was always Boys, who'd seen me once Peeping out from her wagon. I felt her hesitate as he picked me up, then swiftly hid me behind his Back, but she was swift & threw him an apple, shouted *Catch!*

By the Tail-end of 1868, Custer's Civil War Glory had faded in the Shadow of what the Settler-Flesh described as the Indian Wars. What a sordid joke. In any case, Washita was a battle Eliza knew little of in any version of material Truth. Custer arrived back, his Snake-Eyes darting like a Lizard's Tongue & tossed her a Bison blanket as a souvenir. Once I got Whiff of it, I was aware, if not of the Mind-opening future that lay before me, then of the scale of the Staggering atrocities that trailed behind our Bloodthirsty, onion-Breathed leader.

Now, it is vital to enunciate that a Doll will always yearn for the bonding that comes with an attachment to an infant Soft-Flesh.

& Also factual, that a Doll's life can change in an instant—as we are lost & found & dangled & dropped. & This more so for a Rag-Clan-Mannequin such as I, with our innate attraction as Creatures of cloth & straw & Horse-Hair (particularly, as explicated, to the Canine-Quadruped) & our ability to absorb & transmit memory with every scent & scene encountered, whether grounded on the Earth Plane or in the ether of night.

You see a Damsel can detect the unfamiliar Pheromones of another. It is a shudder of deep knowing that is confounded & troublesome to dismiss. It gnaws at the Trunks & Valves & other chewy bits of the Heart as a Rat gnaws at the rotting Toes of Dead-Flesh on the battlefield. It aches & burns at the back of the Eyeball, as if that jellyish orb had been gouged & pecked from its gaping Socket by a murder of ravenous Crows.

& So, alas, it was for Libbie, who followed her Husband to the ends of what she considered to be the civilised Earth & back, so she might prevent another of his increasingly frequent, barely concealed & consistently denied infidelities.

Certainly, she had felt her Beloved's mind wander to Eliza's uppity Behind, which could be glimpsed on occasion through the flaps as the teenager disrobed hurriedly in her tent. It was a fantasy Libbie found easy enough to intercept by the simplest of offerings that could be made by a Soft-Flesh of either sex, although it was somewhat disconcerting as the Dogs would invariably set to a cacophonous Howling whenever she presented on all Fours.

Eliza, as enunciated, was aware of the General's myriad 'passions' & made it her business to exploit these tendencies as a weakness rather than a danger. & Thus, despite the apparent delusion of her gambit, it became something of a game between them, where the threat to fling her across his Knee & spank her Butt with The Old Lady's Hairbrush for such & such wretched impertinence was met with a look so unamused it could have curdled milk in the Udder. At times Eliza pushed back perilously hard, telling the General, in no uncertain terms, she wouldn't give the likes of him a second glance if he was the last Soft-Flesh on God's lush & green-leafed earth & that she was going to find herself a Man, a *real* Man with prospects, a Judge, or failing that, a Lawyer. Which, as it happens, in her happy ending, she did. Surprisingly, for the most part she got clean away with it: folding truth into a wobbling soufflé of steaming Pony-excrement with deft assurance.

Regardless that the tightrope on which era & circumstance had forced her to teeter was precarious, Eliza had learnt that aggression was also flirtation & that flirtation, for such a man as Custer, was always a fruitful flattery. For in all interactions with powerful White-Flesh a degree of Brown-Nosing was required.

But this morning, Eliza was in a bad mood. Libbie had been in foul fettle ever since her Husband had returned from Washita, an expedition on which she had not accompanied him. News around an army campfire travels like smoke, sometimes its fumes come with the appetising curl of Cartilage melting, of Beef stew, or Sausage, Egg & of course Onions frying, at others its announcements are acrid. It was not *what* was said on this occasion, which Libbie knew would be a version of the Truth, but what was *not* said. Custer's younger brother Tom was sporting a Shiner & although the fact that the ever-competing siblings has been fighting, the subject as to what it had been *about* had been more elusive. The facts emerged, slowly, as steam hissed & shook the lid of Eliza's camp kettle. Yes, Female-Flesh was a known Spoil of War, which army Wives took care to overlook. But there was something in the speed & brightness which this & that Cavalryman spoke about the weather & the subsequent bobbing of her Husband's Adam's Apple combined with Tom's unusually sullen demeanour that alerted Libbie to the fact that this situation was different.

On top of these tightly coiled tensions, was an early-morning tussle with the Quadruped Pack. It was not, as one might expect that cursed & cunning Byron who delivered me that morning at the tip-tappity Feet of the General, who sat by the campfire, polishing the brass buttons on his top coat & Whistling through his Blistered Lips, his Tongue surreptitiously licking a seep of Pus from the rugged crater of a burst Coldsore. Although it was he, Byron, who had snuffled my right Hip from underneath Eliza's pillow. I hadn't spent more than a minute clenched between his sharp, pointed Incisors when that scoundrel Stag-Hound which answered to the name of Blucher, snatched me from under Byron's quivering Nose & Whiskers, which had discerned a large & somewhat festering morsel of Mule-offal & dropped me Absent-mindedly so as to chow down upon it. It was this pungent, olfactory distraction that saved me being torn from Torso to shoelace in the fray that ensued: Blucher's growls rumbling through my churning Tummy as I exited the dark & shadowy corners of Eliza's tent.

*Well, well, whassat ya got there, Bloocher?! Sure as hell don't look like one ah Byron's Bunny-Rabbits* the General exclaimed, stretching out a cold, yet oddly clammy Hand—From my supine position I witnessed the subtle yet habitual twitch in his Groin travel upwards to the Spittle-flicked ends of his gingery-blond Moustache.

On this occasion, however, Libbie, who had bitten her Bottom Lip until it swelled in a bid to suppress her fury at Custer's growing affections for his Red-Flesh Baby-Mother *Monah-setah* as he called her, whose name she'd heard whispered & shushed, swooped at the opportunity to displace the rage she carried on her Shoulder like a pickaxe.

Knowing that I was a Beloved-Mannequin of some significance, she released her arrow from the quiver with a spontaneous flourish. *Oh, for Heaven's sake, Autie!* she'd exclaimed as he shook her like crumbs from a tablecloth from her perch upon his Lap, leaning forward as he did so to scoop me up from the ashes onto which his third-favourite Pooch had deposited my twisted Physique. *What in God's name are you gonna do with that ugly, black, Thing? It's abominable!* she screeched. *In fact why don't you give it to that Squaw you've been fucking's bastard Brat?*

The General Eyed her for a moment, the tips of his Moustache bristling slightly *You know, my dear Little Army Crow* he countered *I may do just that.*

# LADY MAMIKO

Maman never tires
of brushing my jet-black hair—
which is quite tiresome.


Her bedroom door
creaks loud as wind in the trees
down in Central Park.


Subterfuge is hard
enough already: Princes
are quite obsessive.

We managed to coax Maman out of her dressing room back
to Japan Town. She popped me in a pram next to Malibu Barbie
and wheeled us down the hallway. I've no idea what she was
doing in there. I think they had a big night in Barbieville and she
was sleeping off a hangover. It's quite dark because the lightbulb
outside the Music Room has blown and it's an interior corridor
so Maman stops at the pantry to light a stubby candle in a silver

holder. It's quite heavy so her wrist shakes a little and wax drips onto the pram's coverlet. Luckily she didn't notice otherwise it'd be another twenty minutes for her to wander back and then forget what she came for.

# CHRISTIE BARBIE

Acid. LSD. '68 was a haze    of tear gas, hash: Leb &
Black    All us cats   wore     their berets   tilted

Che Guevara style. We were sistahs of the revolution,   you
dig?  I joined an ashram, sat cross legged, I was gonna

eat brown rice forever same way  Maman only ate  tinned
fish and crackers    She coulda dined     on a dozen

golden eggs by Fabergé a day  Not mash potato in a
hospital canteen  or surviving on one yoghurt

I just wish she'd donated to a real cause not bought
jewellery she never wore nowhere,  I'm a chick rocks a

kaftan!  I taught Maman   meditation    Peace &
Love    She was into it long as no stud wanted to feel

more than her mind    Not her crocodile wallet
neither  We had sexual liberation,        free love

open    relationships    not Maman, uh-uh, she
preferred    life alone, indoors  getting lost in time & space

quietly building  Japanese castles, elaborate mazes, this
rabbit warren    went so far down  the helter

skelter, Jack Kerouac skidded offa that freeway ya feel?
Therapy coulda helped   I mean a daddy so rich with no

understanding.  He was one motherfucking   bad
vibes honky  who hustled his seat in the Senate

Watts burns they call it riots  Civil Rights?!  Malcolm
X was assassinated by the C-I-A Vietnam, Napalm & Maman's

yearning for her Mama on harp!  I played her Alice Coltrane:
zero interest!   Jeez, she chic    but she sure ain't hip

# LADY MAMIKO

I'm a bit obsessed
with the way shadows fall on
the folds of my dress.

With the way shadows
loom and flicker as Maman
scatters confetti.

With the way shadows
darken and illuminate
words we dare not speak.

Last night was endless—
there is nothing so thrilling
as an unsheathed sword!

The rustle of silk
behind paper screens: a gasp
is such extravagance.

When we get back from Maman's quarters rehearsals are already under way. Malibu Barbie fell asleep again and when she wakes up she seems quite disorientated. She stares round at the room rubbing her eyes and then snuggles back in for another nap next to Squirrel Nutkin who wraps his bushy tail round her neck like one of Maman's fox-fur stoles. Nobody wears those any more but they used to be quite popular, their taxidermied snouts draping along behind the lady.

> Hikaru holds his
> father's parasol up high—
> the Emperor stands tall.

> Who shares an Empress
> when the Emperor still lives?
> A young prince must shine.

Hikaru gestures for me to come and join him on the stage. Maman is rummaging under the pagoda roof. I've no idea what she's looking for and neither does she.

> The Emperor loves
> our Yozakura parties.
> Their abundant blooms!

> Seating arrangements
> are so hard this year.
> So too Hikaru.

Yesterday evening
he brought a red peony—
as did My Lady.

Two look quite perfect
in my little lacquered vase.
Three topple over!

# MALIBU BARBIE

Astral travel  is real.    Night times   we rode
bareback &  naked,        me        & lil Maman

clutching      .  the waves' silvery    manes while
dolphins sang with ecstatic whales!

Every full moon we'd drift off      go swimming
free &   careless, wild    dreams we

guzzled like  Mai Tai's    while Dolly swooned over
handsome Sam  That cute   Hawaii boy Maman loved

in the days when her hair was  lustrous  & he was
junior surf    champion  He was her first

kiss!    Me, I keep my transistor   blaring loud as a
lifeguard's      jacket, grab my  spare bikini    head for

Malibu in the buggy, count waves   while a gnarly
night nurse   flicks through Maman's *Vanity Fair*

or tweaks the dials till  her eyeballs flicker like a
pinball machine and we're  skinny dipping, which was

quite the thing  back when Maman had fun in the
Roaring Twenties    which were like totally decadent!

Sam was different   He'd sing, stroke her neck
twirl her salty hair in his  fingers  Dude had a strong

undertow it could pull you under but he held her
virginal hand in his and I'm not gonna lie there

was hope      of a   new life,  a passport   but it was
exhilarating, romantic!    He'd serenade her on his

yukulele That brown boy  had talent  which was worth
zilch cos her Papa never did fix it with immigration

# LADY MAMIKO

Maman draws Manga
characters well now: the eyes
are the hardest part.

Hikaru makes an excellent model. He actually has the same
eyes as his character in the film, big and appealing and glassy. It
is one of his most endearing features. I don't tell him this: his ego
and his eyes are about the same size.

It's natural to
want to spend time with me—but
I'm very busy!

I received several invitations this week, some business, some
pleasure. Some I shall accept, some I shall decline. I ought to
practise my calligraphy. I ought to nudge Maman about ink and
maybe even blossom. I wonder if we might get her to get phone
Macy's. She's become awkward about even receiving deliveries
these days now Lisette is gone. Her crackers are stale and she has
trouble opening tins.

The Art of Bonsai
is attention to detail.
And a steady hand.

The Scholar scribbles
me a new note: my lilac
is indeed fragrant.

My Lady tells me
Hikaru loves the garden—
its shaded corners.

Can she not see he is only being so attentive to her to annoy me?
This is how he operates and I thought she would have been able to
see through this smokescreen, it is utterly translucent.

Outside in the park
the sky floats on the lake—here
a telephone rings.

# DOLLY

Normalement Maman answers le telephone ring
as it is more instantaneous quick
than a letter which is not la même chose as talk
and not keeping her from pleasurable things
such as listening to records of violin
concerto Stradivarius or speaking to check
doll dresses at Christian Dior as le fabric
must be absolument correct, satin
especially or it could fall wrong, or worse dégueulasse!

Specifications accurate are essential bien sur
for all Maman's projects architectural
which are numerous and tres tres complex.
Imagine if Le Hirosaki Palace measurement
or Hokkaido Tea Room is wrong size or scale.

If Hokkaido Tea Room is wrong scale or size
Maman is agitated most extreme.
When furnitures is articulated 'green
lacquer' and 'mock bamboo' for chaises and side
table and golden sheets pour le deep frieze
wallpaper this is exact what Maman mean.

Simples. But it is strange, as deep hidden
is our telephone number, only those long inside
know how to reach us and less now she suffers bad ears
and does not want artificial sound machine
when she is calling Mister Subaru-Artist.

Normally it is only possible Madame Pierre
who is recently widow and bonne amie
best-friend lady strong in giving all advices

All advices given by Maman's lady best-friend
are strong and medical and this is why
she is capable to dial-in and then Le Docteur dies
and Maman has no physician, Madame P no husband
more alive than the wall-mounted stag's head
above the tall umbrella stand carved in ivory.
He is not curing carcinoma-nasty and Dolly
is thinking if he lives longer Maman would dead
too. Alors. Voila! Dolly must manifest
all dolls seated in front row chairs avec aussi
les animals: le tabby-cat Muschkin and kitten,

five white poodles, Delphine-Jumeau's Pekinese (best
in show), the groom, footman, carriage horses
to explain them how we must prepare for all things.

To explain them how we must for all things prepare
Dolly makes assembly beneath le disco
glitter ball and laser light in Barbieville so
all dolls can hear les bulletins from dancefloor speaker.

DJ Kenny Ken is pulling up in le sports car
Ferrari on passenger side wearing day-glo
shorts and Ray Ban lunettes sitting next to
Scientist Barbie's petite soeur French Teacher.

She is no more French than her cheap pencil skirt!
Putaine! Excuse-moi, mais Dolly is not Saint
Joan or any other and even concepts
most basic this Vinyl cannot comprehend a word.
And it is better Dolly speaks not of her accent
nor driving style which is hazard when best.

Oui, this driving is haphazard at the least
and since when is French-Teacher affording stallion
vehicle with adjustable seats? And this when Maman
is barely able to swallow morsel to eat?

Dépêche-toi! We are waiting for Scientist Barbie
to arrive avec les tests results for Cherry Blossom
but DJ Kenny Ken is ordering champagne
and not obeying when Dolly does request
nicely. Also absent is most vital
element Le Général: who is special brain
power on how to keep our Maman alive.

Dolly must be more patient than the rose petal
about to unfurl after sun breaks through rain
clouds skittering across dark moody sky.

# STARS 'N' STRIPES BARBIE

And when the saints, and when the—Army life is
battle and brawn   Lacing up my combats ready for  War!

Camouflage is de rigueur   Gotta know who you fighting for
Doing my duty, dodging bullets, diddling squats   I'm

elite task force   What I don't know's classified    Put one
foot down, then the other        Don't go slinging hand

grenades or you gon lose an arm, a leg & your dinky china
head … You know where I learnt    to master   POW

interrogation?  This here soldier was deep in the
jungle   on a special forces missive  when the Viet Cong

kidnapped me from behind the the sofa    Weren't no
love spared between us I'll tell ya that for nothing!

Madame Butterfly,  Miss Saigon  We all had codenames in
Nam!    Hup, two, three, four! Helicopter blades spinning …

Operation Cherry had me for dead   Now Dolly's got
PTSD, mumbling Hiroshima, Nagasaki, Pearl Harbor: I

quizzed her so hard she tripped out on Blossom & hit
rock bottom   We all paid the price   each n every  last

soldier   I'm a Stars 'n' Stripes Special   No reign of
terror  lasts   Fear's        a soldier  wears one tatty

uniform   But when you're beat   you're beat   Not every
veteran  gets a V-day parade   Hell, we got ourselves a new

world order!   Dolly wants to wave her white knickers  as an
exit strategy—kiss my ass!   I'm like Missy, are you

yanking my chain?  This is a skirmish You can't
zone out now honeybun   We jus' stocked up on ammunition

# THE GENERAL

*Reminiscences & Recollections of General Obadiah*
*Louverture Little Rock Yellow Bird Junior the Second*

## A MEMOIR

Yellow Bird was dragged out of his mother's Uterus by the Ankles, his scrunched Hands & tiny Fingernails reaching back to whence he came.

Now, it is vital to enunciate that a Doll will always yearn for the bonding that comes with an attachment to an infant Soft-Flesh. However, while a Doll *desires* a sense of Oneness that is prevalent when bonded with a Child-Flesh, it is nonetheless a hazardous business. My time with Yellow Bird was no exception. Being dragged hither & thither by the Arm, Hair, Neck or Throat was commonplace, if objectionable. Mud was also a feature. As was the Puddle, Dust, Poo, Wee, Vomit, Snot & Donkey-Dung. Many indignities are suffered, but it is both duty & honour to serve in this manner.

Of course, Yellow Bird's mother, my beloved Meyouzah, also required my assistance, for barely a Moon passed, full or sickle, without an Eye-Flickering revival of her violet traumas, whether physical or astral. Custer had taken her captive at Washita in 1868, along with fifty-three others. It was a battle in which both her Father, Little Rock, who I never met, but whose name I bear, & her younger Brother, Hawk, who had just turned fourteen, had been slaughtered. All of them had survived the massacre at Sand Creek, almost exactly four years earlier & it had left its Scars, deep within her Flesh & Ethereal Body.

Those days she would cling to me hard & I would attempt to calm the erratic thump-ity thump of her Heart, that pounded with the grief of losing her father & little brother. Many Tears were shed, of sorrow & rage & I absorbed them with a puff of my tightly stuffed Chest, proud as any farmyard Cockadoodle to assist in this crystalline purification that is the work of all who toil & labour in the Mannequin-Realm. Her dreams were lurid & insistent, as the Ancestors endeavoured to help her ravaged, yet beautiful Body process what her Brain could not.

*SAND CREEK, NOVEMBER 1864*
*Waves of white, thick like the blizzard that swirled in the sky. It was winter & our breath was a cloud of white above our heads. The ponies were tired. The dogs were tired. My father was tired. Tired of making peace with White-Flesh who would break our Bones & our Skulls easy & as often as they did their word. We slept together for warmth & to gather our strength.*

This is what Meyouzah told me. Not in words, but in dreams I was encumbent to transmit. This is what she told her Son, Yellow Bird, whose name I also carry, whose Intimate-Inanimate I had become. He, who, like his mother was noble of Blood & Heart & dazzling of Smile.

Meyouzah slept under a Buffalo blanket, a Pelt wrested from

a Beast her father Little Rock hunted & skinned & her mother Skunk-Woman had tanned & stretched & smoothed flat with a carefully selected rock. Its Hide held dreams & nightmares & the echo of a thousand thundering Hooves. Memories too. Of another dread night, a dark night of dim moon. On barren land the White-Flesh had 'allocated' to the tribe.

Black Kettle had been promised peace, he had been promised provisions, he had been promised safe passage for his people on their own lands & he flew their America flag & the white one too as instructed, but the White-Flesh sent Barbarians instead.

Bloodthirsty Men; Soldiers only in name, Rabid Men who came & slashed: slashed babies from Bellies with sabres, sabres gleaming with Blood. Sabres sharp enough to slice Veins from pulsing Corpses, sharp enough to Scalp a thousand Skulls. Scalps that were brandished as trophies at Denver Opera House while the orchestra played & petulant Ladies waved fans to cool their flushed & pink-Cheeked Faces.

Oh yes, sweet, innocent Friend, this massacre was high art! A plump tobacco pouch was fashioned from Magpie's cousin's Breast; a purse for plundered gold was stitched from an old man's Testes—they had to pull the Leathery, dried Flesh hard to smooth the Wrinkles out.

& Those of Squeamish Stomach might now their Eyes avert, for I must speak account. To tell of how the air shuddered with the musk of Gall & Guts as they slit Noses, Lips & Labia, Clitoris & other parts of Genitalia—that they did stretch across saddle bows & tasselled hats or mount on sticks like lollipops—as the marching band rode out, playing one of those Godawful ditties, triumphant behind their leader, Chivington. Chivington & I shall say his name this once again, Chivington, to damn him further down. The officer who claimed to kill five hundred fighting Men but told that ragtag band of ruffians to *Kill and Scalp them all—big and little; for it's Nits make Lice.*

& This is what she told me. My Meyouzah: the girl the White-Flesh called Monasetah or Sallie-Ann. Some said it meant Gone by Sunset, but, she told me, her true name was really Morning Walker. My Meyouzah, who was no more than seventeen, who survived the atrocities at Sand Creek, only to be captured & abused again.

White Buffalo Calf Woman, Spirit-Prophet of the Lakota, spoke to Meyouzah many times in her dreams. Meyouzah listened, Meyouzah watched, but—She could never remember what was said in a way that was exact. White Buffalo Calf Woman's visions of warning wafted over her head. These words puffed out of her Mouth, like smoke from her pipe, big fluffy clouds of smoke, smoke that turned to clouds, clouds that scudded & skipped, clouds that clustered in herds of white Buffalo that rushed across the plains, choo-chooing like a train on its silvery track. Meyouzah aimed her arrow at the Buffalo Skull, right between the bridge of the Nose & fired & her aim was true. But for every Beast she shot, clean between the Eyes, another two popped up. & Every time she shot two, three more thundered along, Etc, Etc.

While many aspects of these lunar visions—for Meyouzah dreamt deepest when the moon was new or full—were Head-scratchingly tricksy to interpret, this particular motif was obvious to divine. It was the reason her father, Little Rock, stood by his friend Black Kettle. It was the reason why both chiefs preached peace over war with the White-Settler-Flesh: for every day more of them appeared on the horizon with their laws & treaties & acts, each day there were more of them, with their Articles, bullets & maps.

Yes, this is what she told me. My Meyouzah. & This was how it was. It was the time when the White-Flesh make their Thanksgiving, with Wild-Turkey-Flesh & pumpkin. It was the time when the veil between Spirit & Skin was thin & the wind blew icy & snow drifted out & in. Dreams pungent with gun-smoke spiralling into Screams that rang out, stark against the quiet of snowfall, stark as the splatter of scarlet on white. Dreams I came also to inhabit, dreams it was my job to slip over my Sheep's-Wool-Head & into my Mind-Eye, visions that were hard to decipher & harder to ignore.

Hazy shimmerings Meyouzah's mother, Skunk-Woman, would have to shake her out of, lest she get lost in the labyrinthine lanes & alleys of the Other-world. Nightmares Meyouzah alone could ride Bareback across the grassy plains, holding tight as the visions galloped & reared. Dreams that reeked of Urine that coursed through the village as the ghosts of slaughtered Toddle-Flesh piddled with fear. Dreams where her mother yanked her by the Hair & her Plaits wriggled into Grass-Snakes that hissed & writhed. Dreams where they crawled across stony, frozen ground on their Stomachs to hide. Dreams where White Buffalo Calf Woman wrapped Meyouzah & Skunk-Woman in her white blanket so they too were white against the snow, white & invisible under her downy coat, unseen by the Soldiers who shot, stabbed, gutted & slit.

That this Oracle visited Meyouzah at all was a mystery & one which Skunk-Woman did not prod too deep. Skunk-Woman ascribed her daughter's inability to interpret White Buffalo Calf Woman's soothsaying to the fact that as a Shahiyela, or as the White-Flesh called it, Cheyenne, her access to the Lakota shimmerings was limited. Many of the Shahiyela were Mixed-Blood Lakota & many of the Lakota were part-Shahiyela. Tall Bull, a leader of the rebel Dog Soldiers, amongst them. Buried in the pit of her Stomach & the grit of her Wisdom-Teeth was the knowledge that her Daughter, like so many of the Clan, was no longer sure of Little Rock, not so much as a Father, but as a Man. Waving the White Flag for the White-Flesh as had Black Kettle would come to no good.

## WASHITA, NOVEMBER 1868

When a Seance Bébé wants to reach deep in the heart of a Soft-Flesh, a known technique is to activate the sense of Smell. For it is the aroma of a favourite dinner, of Meat & Marrow softly disintegrating into a stew, or a first kiss recalled by the half-remembered trail of honeysuckle on a sultry summer's eve, that draws back the curtain on the stage of memory. Yes, there is a certain drama, nostalgia even. The theatre of death is real & pungent.

& Yet there are times when the *absence* of an aroma is almost as powerful as its presence. Thus, I refer you to the crisp, white, almost imperceptible odour of snow. For snow, still crusted, delicate & virgin, never fails to provoke the shudder that courses through the aperture of every stitch, that trembles at the very core of my Rag-Mannequin Being.

Snow fell that night, on the banks of the River Washita, at the end of November, 1868. It was a foot thick on the ground. & It was icy. & Bitter. & Custer's men were cold & bitter. & Custer too was bitter. Bitter & ready to exact revenge through conquest & slaughter. Revenge on any Human-Flesh or Beast he thought might block his ascension through the competitive jostle of political skulduggery. Still smarting from a Court Martial & anxious to prove himself again to the grandees of a government that simultaneously rewarded & reprimanded the thrust of a hard-Nosed &

dedicated Sadist. For despite his Boyish ways & japes, Custer was a Creature of Machiavellian bent, who took some pleasure in the Art of Discipline. In making his Men, Saddlesore & chilled to the Skeleton, dismount & continue the day's journey on unshod, chilblained Feet, simply for the so-called crime of complaining under their Breath.

On that snowy night there was a bright star in the sky & Custer took this astronomical phenomenon as his Omen of good luck.

The White-Flesh soldiers crept over the hillside to surround the village. Custer's second favourite Staghound had to be strangled—& a little Mongrel-Terrier too. An obedient Hand clasped her juddering Jaw & tightened the lariat. Tightened the noose round her furry Windpipe until her brown beseeching Eyes bulged, her tongue lolled & her Bowel dilated, lest she let loose a telltale Whimper & set the village Dogs to barking.

As usual Custer had dressed for the occasion. He fancied himself an Eagle-Feather Brave as he led his brass-buttoned troops to attack a lightly vibrating huddle of Soft-Flesh Mothers & Babes. Babes nuzzled at the Breast, cuddled close & spoony in their teepees for warmth as their Breath plumed into the freezing dark.

It took Custer's men a little more than an hour to slaughter some 700 Horses, Mules & stumbling Foals. There were other seized provisions too, the partial inventory of which includes 241 saddles, 573 Buffalo robes, 75 spears, 4,000 arrows & Heads, 210 axes & 140 hatchets, hatchets that would wait, patiently, to be buried at Little Bighorn. Always the history books talk about these Ponies. Custer's orders had been to kill the Men, the Warriors & capture the Women & the Children. Fifty-three survived the onslaught, though they were now Father, Son, Uncle & Brother-less. Orphans & Widows. Black Kettle & his wife Medicine Woman were shot in the back as they fled into the freezing waters of the river. Meyouzah's father Little Rock was Scalped. Hawk, her little Brother, died too. The captives were driven, like Cattle to the Camp. It was a stark yet familiar trauma.

& When night fell again, treacherous with the stink of Entrails, Shit & Innards, the Soldiers set about the Rape that followed Pillage.

# SWISS BARBIE

Alpine meadows, muesli for
        breakfast, my house has a

cuckoo clock out front & our
        dog's a friendly St Bernard.

Either side of a rather high
        fence is where you'll find me.

German or French, we can
        help you in both languages

if you've money to invest.
        Jewels R Us! Joking aside we

keep up with all the very
        latest tech & what's

more important than being
        neutral? Every good

oligarch needs uncrackable
          passwords, our client base is

royalty & crooks. I'm an old
          style chalet girl, finishing school

type, so your secrets are our
          utmost priority & well, the

vaults speak for themselves.
          Whenever you're ready I'm here.

XXX Let's catch up when you're in
          Zurich!  Love you! It's been real.

# LADY MAMIKO

Hikaru Genji
enters without knocking first!
Sneaks up from behind.

My cheeks flush, tremble
with a delicious
anticipation.

> A lady would have
> sent him away. My Lady
> has sent him my way.

Does she want to test
my loyalty? Surely not.
She knows I have none.

> Hikaru Genji
> is an adequate lover.
> My Lady, sublime.

Tonight his hair smells
of something familiar.
I can't quite place it.

>         We kiss, then I gasp
>         when my mouth is empty, gasp
>         when he spills the beans.

His confession is
more intimate, strange: perhaps
he's feeling guilty.

# PARISIAN BARBIE

Actually there's more to me than
berets & baguettes: I worship a

Creole Goddess, our Black Venus
dancing in a banana-skin skirt whose

égalité went up in flames in Missouri, the
French Resistance was a safer space, La

Guerre was everywhere, as it is here.
How many dolls have to suffer &

in the name of who, or what?
Josephine Baker was a thirteen-year-old

kid when she got hitched—was it
love? Who knows? She was on her second

marriage by the time she was fifteen. La Revue
Negre was her big break. In Paris.

Obviously I wasn't good enough for the
porcelain gang which was no love lost.

Quite the opposite. As Groucho Marx said, I
refuse to join any club that would have me.

Stereotypes were outré at the fin de siècle.
The good Général & I are compatriots.

Underground Resistance is necessary—I'm
Vinyl & Proud!   I've friends in every

walk of life, rags & riches, we tried a
pax, but Dolly won't give up until the Barbies

yield so I said go do your song & dance with the
Ziegfeld Follies, it's over cherie, I'm getting out.

# DOLLY

Chère Maman, each day she is more fragile.
Monsieur le Docteur believes her allergic
to soleil! Her skin is white-china-like
and I am knowing every new wrinkle.
You see we porcelains think alone mais feel
as one, as raindrops trickle to the creek.
This is why we are more supèrieure than plastique:
everyone knows the Barbies like to make meal

of everything, I hear this from Le Général direct . . .
their favourite food style is le saucisson
most obvious, apparently—they gyrate to boom-box
bang-bang, hip-hop, disco electrified
noises, chattering like les spoons in a saucepan
in their polka-dot bikini pom poms!

Pom pom! Dans la bikini polka dot
cerises, just as my Cherry Blossom Powder
brings a charm to existence, je ne sais how!
There are things we know and things we do not.
Barbie-Scientist unbuttons her blanc coat
and I explain her how much nicer is chamber

music of Paganini or the other, Brahms
but she is telling me only she is *soooo hot*

will I be so *enchanting* and to *please bring*
*her a Long Island Ice Tea—in a big, talllllll*
*glass, cos that's how she likes her*—then she makes pause
and I am about to—but she says *virgin*
*of course* as if Dolly offers alcohol—
mais I am tres polite and agree *of course!*

Je suis so polite and agree *bien sur* mais
when I am returning back from our parlour
Barbie-Scientist is on the other
side of the sofa, her hair in splayed
bun when before she wears—how is it you say? —
bunches, which is big mistake, quelle horreur
this hair style and she who is so clever
with papers from Einstein Université

to prove it! Unlike Barbie Rendezvous-
sur-la-Plage who is making degree class in aerobic
body pump with Bondai-Kenny in red jeep
vehicle each Saturday afternoon.
For this game Dolly is too claustrophobic
and afterwards anyway they must make like sleep.

When Maman is sleeping is when I speak
dans her good ear, possibly a whisper
is enough for Dolly to charisma
and warn so she is understanding each

importance *sufficement*, there can be no weak
links in this jewelled charm bracelet, Cartier
love heart ou non! This deep terrain is a matter
most mountainous, its shadowy peak dark
and glooming where danger is every place
unexpected and seemingly innocent!

Remember, j'éxpliqué Maman, how even
our best friend drops A-bomb from military base
in big mushroom, boom! Though this is incorrect
Le Général explains me, as it was *we* America did *nuke* Japan.

Le Général, I explain *him*, how it was anyway Japan
began this abomination, and also how Tokyo
Ladies and Lords in eyelash-soft Kyoto
silk fineries fluttering behind painted fans
was also suffering after GI-Joe-War under American
changes to aristocratiques, so Fuji-Ko
and Ume-Ko Princesses now take no
special appellation—just Wisteria and Plum plain.

Lady Mamiko is also strong caring
over Maman's Chrysanthemum Castle
and all our Fifth Avenue minuscules
and is tres tres occupé avec preparing
for the springtime festival pour Hina doll
dans our exquisite oriental citadel.

Our oriental citadel is most exquisite
and furnished just so! Its tea rooms and temples

authentic as any Jumeau doll's dimples
or antique lace bloomers and bonnet.
Sushi and sashimi with chopsticks
are laid out on crimson linen, most ample
with pink shrimps for the Emperor to sample
who is making special imperial visit.

Lady Mamiko is overseeing matters
of all tradition and decorum
avec attentions precise as the sash
on a stiff-sleeved kimono of Onnagata
– which is fine gentlemen
who is dressing more ladylike than geisha.

More ladylike than geisha is Maman
now she stays behind our apartment doors
of which there are at least forty-two on both floors
twelve and eight. This, Lady Mamiko say is deep problem
pour Maman when she lived avec Monsieur Husband.
Mais, I am correcting to blush, it is an era
now when too many things are peculiar
and we must concentrate absolument on Blossom

Powder as this is our only lucky solution.
Maman is thin as a spindly Louis Quinze
table leg and her bottom lip disappears!
Quelle catastrophe! Soon she will be gone!
Pouf! Like Anna-Maman's sapphires from CitiBank!
Lost under her fluffy cardigans cashmere.

These sapphires rest on the cashmere jumper
of another femme! So many eras gone but Maman was afraid
there would be more gossip salacious with bad
photograph in cloche hat and fox fur.

This she did speak seulement to Madame Pierre
while straightening on her lapel an orchid
which bien sur is exactement à la mode.
But Dolly is not stupid – this medical shrieks disaster!

Le Général is advising Dolly to calm:
he is communing with Barbie Scientist
on chemical lab business daily and can discover more
each nights about Special Operation Blossom:
he is speaking it goose-feather soft, like military
secret, hush hush, nothing to worry for!

Hush hush, this secret is le super worry
for Dolly as she is observing bad circumstance
over Maman's face which could soon collapse
and is making some contortion already!

Poor Maman, she is not like Dolly
whose emptiness is delightful once
you become accustom to constant sense
of dew-fresh youth, never to make elderly.

Last night Dolly squeezes Cherry Powder tube
so hard and there is hardly ointment enough
and when I go looking for what Scientist Barbie

promises in her boudoir she is quite nude
and is maximum cross that Dolly interrupt
she and Student Barbie experiment lab test.

Dans l'experiment lab test Student Barbie
is dressed only in le fish-net stockings
and is riding palomino rocking
horse bareback which is not quite elegant
to say least, mais Dolly has no time for argument
and is not mentioning how cigar smoking
in official chemical laboratoire is not joke
material as Maman's visage is urgent
and she is baring teeths through her left cheek
more fierce than black fangs of le polar bear
skin rug on which is lying Master of the Hunt
in bright red jacket in front of sparking onyx
mantelpiece. Pah! These Barbarian Vinyl Faces are careless!
We must replace le fire guard immédiatement.

Immédiatement we replace le fire guard
Le Général is arriving utterly unannounced when
normally at this hour he is already gone
to pluck banjo music or write new words
for songs after church or when we play card
games such as tarot or belote in le Salon.
Le Général is having surprise too as Maman
requires often Dolly at this hour, mais he is glad
he is finding me here finally which is un peu
télépathique because Dolly is telling no one

of her arrangement or plans to visit
as this is absolute emergency, mon dieu!

If Dolly is not making scheme for Maman
no doll or figurine is safe, neither bisque nor plastic.

No doll or figurine is safe neither plastic nor bisque
when Shit-Bank—merde! They refuse to pay
no more than three million half—voleurs!—on Monday
Maman receives this papier de toilette cheque
after beaucoup legal correspondence: such illicit
business for all who make le monnaie
of Cartier blue-diamond jewels to brass alchemy
baksheesh sorcerer style! And are having no fright or risk.

When Dolly looks to le Britannicas
Encyclopedia-Reference for authority
of medicine and other irrelevances
its knowledge is small as a *keshi-bina*
doll mouth—which is le maximum tiny
as carcinoma-nasty is immense.

Le carcinoma-nasty is an immense
iceberg capable to sink *Le Titanic*
avec le gnashing shark jaws gigantic
that did swallow Maman's poor defenceless
cousin Walter who is drowning amongst
the freezy waves of l'Ocean Atlantique
on a ship for which Anna-Maman et Papa buys tickets

for la famille entire as tourist event
of new twentieth century! Dolly is invited
to accompany Maman as companion
best-friend, second only to her beloved Andrée.
Everybody was bien super excited
to take this iceberg disaster ship company
return journey. Pouf! It is a miracle to save Maman that day!

To save Maman again this day is a miracle
us dolls are requiring: Dolly makes
pink potion thick and fluffy strawberry milkshake
style from le petit pewter crucible
with powder puff mais supplies are critical
low and Scientist Barbie—is too long time to take
and if Dolly did have neurology this headache
would be zap like lightning oracle
from where we must find our future answer.
Lady Mamiko is preferring I-Ching
of China, pouf! For this Dolly is taking no advices
on unknown soothsayer random factor!
On this occasion we must begs Miss Ting
for tea leaves reading. We take no chances.

# NIGERIAN BARBIE

Arms dealing? If you want AK-47s try the
Brits! I told Dolly, they'll do anything for

Cherry though obviously if we're talking
dollars then my best friend's cousin went to

Eton, so he's got connections, a boy who
fagged for him, unofficial of course, a

gentleman's agreement, don't trust a
Harrovian whatever you do, y'know guys & their

incendiary devices! I cook the absolute best
Jollof rice, my aunty's married to the

King of Benin & I got the recipe from her.
Lagos is obviously the financial centre &

military HQ, and anyway it's also West Africa's
nightlife capital, so it makes perfect sense for

Oxbridge types in the City, you know my fiancé
Peregrine, right? He's got a PhD & he's a

Quant at one of the Big Three, I think he can
raise enough capital to buy Dolly out, he's a

smooth operator—yah, I know, my Latin
tutor knew Sade in the '80s, hold on a sec,

um, yeah, sorry gotta take that, I've been
virtually under siege, I've got these Rolex

watches, for the select few, actually they're
ex-display models, totally legit, Swiss Made.

Yinka? Yeah, she knows how to keep it
zipped—this is just between us, you & me.

# MISS TING

Miss Ting did tell

Dolly fi bring anudder cup an' saucer fi read tea leafs. The one Dolly bring too small h'an dainty even if it did carry all di way craass corridor from blossoms festival preparations in Lady Mamiko zen garden where gold an' black koi fish swim in pond clear as hayngel-eyewater.

Miss Ting did tell

lah-di-dah Dolly fi drink up, hold di handle in er lef' han', swirl it tree time, h'anti-clockwise an' think quietly bout serious question a siddung di bottom a her mind-eye, then – an h'only then – to turn 'er cup topsy-turvy pon di gold-rimmed, rose petal, chinee-bone saucer an wait fuh di liquid fi drain out. Aftah we do this, Miss Ting go look fi shapes an' pattern.

Miss Ting did tell

Dolly she see snake, yellow an' black with a cobra head uncoil an' slither in long grass bleach white as geisha-face. Miss Ting also kind enuff to mention how pink petals cascade down from the heavens an' pile up like chicken fedder week before Crismas.

Miss Ting did also tell 'er

'bout how di General go chop di snake with long machete when it crawl up inna Maman face an' out 'er lips an' how it tongue fork an' flicker like flame on a driftwood bonfire. Miss Ting h'also mek articulation 'bout how she shut 'er eye fi catch forty wink while Maman watch kung fu movie with no kung fu for seven thousandth time since we get new video cassette 'bout di bwoy did weep when peach tree cut down by 'im famly.

Maman drop tear from er eye all the way tru this bit, an' the whiteface-geisha onnagata-lady-bwoy dem wearing all kinda big sleeve kimono an' bang gong and pluck mandolin string same way dem carry on a Emperor Hirohito funeral las' year. Inna Miss Ting dream is Dolly who haffi pass tru a shadow dark bamboo grove same as we have back a yard in country but with baby-pink blossom scatter pon floor like innah the TV video.

Is Dolly follow likkle Japan-pickney in a pale green kimono, likkle bell pon 'im foot a-tinkle tinkle same way sweetie lay path tru forest fi Hansel and Gretel. This clue Dolly nah ketch, for is pure witch a nyam pickney reside in sweetie cottage as h'everybody know. When she get to the orchard the Hina-Doll Emperor tell 'er how she mus' listen good to the General when he tell her strategy-plan fi mek sure she go live in hospital two twos an also how the General a sweet bwoy even if time to time him talk the wrong path.

Miss Ting tink this bit not directly fi Dolly but mi tell 'er this likkle piece a news as it sound like a good ting. Me did also recount how the Japan-Lady skin inna the dream field a long grass is tight like doll-face an she no have no wrinkle or fine line like what dem talk 'bout pon di h'Oil a Olay h'advert, but when you look close, up innah di corner, is a black hole deh-de, no eyeball, like skull an' crossbone flutterin' in de wind above pirate ship. Then the Japan-Lady start cry but h'instead a water fall down 'er chalk face is peach tree blossom not cherry in the shape of a teardrop like the one Pierrot Puppet paint pon 'im cheek so. There is annuder bit when Dolly plunge 'er hand in crocus sack that wriggle an' me tell 'er this mean se you nuff buy puss innah bag but Dolly turn 'er head in other direction an' di wind carry Miss Ting word away an jus like innah the dream deh me did know Dolly nah listen cos 'er eye flit crawss the room fi watch moth batter 'gainst red paper lantern instead a pay proper h'attention.

Miss Ting nah tell
    'er how afta each swipe ah di General blade, one snake mek two mek three an' four. How is Maman blue eye stare cold steel stony glass an how di snakes wriggle an' hiss an' 'er face crumble like statue jus' a try stare down Medusa. Or how Medusa dreadlocks go coil roun' Dolly neck an' tighten like python. Miss Ting also refrain from h'explanation 'bout how di Japan-Lady hair pile high wid pretty-pretty jade an' turtle-back comb in exact same style as Lady Mamiko.

Miss Ting did tell
    nuff story bout how tea leaf readin' is a matter of h'interpretation so it nah mean actual death when Maman face appear out the dark in Egyptian mummy sarcophagus floating tru air like a cloud pon Japanese mountain top.

Miss Ting nah tell

Dolly how she see lightnin strike hit di tip a di pagoda in Japan Town next door to Chrysanthemum Castle an' it burn like major arcana Tower tarot card. How in the far far distance it resemble cathedral spire Notre Dame an' is Dolly who fall from top floor winduh. How at di foot is Lady Mamiko—not Dolly—Maman ketch in 'er shaky palm. Dolly h'irritate Miss Ting like milkmaid pullin pon granny-cow udder, but mi cyaan tell er how back a yard we say cow no know dat 'er tail cut, till 'er tail cuttttt! Nah sah, mi nuh have di heart fi tell 'er that.

# BABYSITTER BARBIE

Awwww ... there there hush hush, don't fuss, a
babysitter has a trick or two up her sleeve, ways to

clamp down on toddler riots! Maman was always on a
diet. After dinner  she'd disappear  close the door to her

en suite  & nobody ever said so but I know she had her
fingers down her throat,   always reserved  she

gagged quietly into the toilet bowl   In my book
*How to Lose Weight*  the answer's on page 2  *Don't Eat!*

I'm never hungry, not having a stomach helps—My
job description is printed on the hem of my skirt  so I

know my place:    change diaper, warm bottles, sing a
lullaby, tuck the babies in tight.   I'm no surrogate

Maman, though    More a big sister who's
numb with chores, longing for night,  so I can make it

out & get shit done   away from prying
porcelain eyes   You know, when Maman finally

quit this      overpopulated  labyrinth  every doll was
relieved, secretly    In truth it's a miracle how she

survived so long    Human flesh  deteriorates
Time    divided by    vast Wealth   to the power of

UV exposure    equals a
Venn diagram   occupied by a father who

worshipped   Himself & money    multiplied by an
ex-husband   who craved sex   in the middle

Yikes! No wonder hospital was homely as
Zion: that one small room made her feel like a child

# LADY MAMIKO

Japan Town buzzes
with excitement: our party
takes place this evening.

        The ceremony
        is the same every year.
        Just like the Oscars.

                Red carpet outfits!
                A little too much sake
                loosens tongues and limbs.

When cherry blossom
swirls in the air you know that
someone sighs somewhere.

    My sighs are hardly blissful now. This is because just as the
party started and I was hoping to slip away again Maman came

and found Hikaru and I and presented us with a new scene she wants us to work on. Every day her condition deteriorates and her attention span, like her emaciated body, is frail. I hope this isn't going to take time. I'm not even needed as a speaking part.

> Hikaru was small
> when his mother died: at
> cherry blossom time.

> His father's new wife
> The Empress is also quite
> young and exquisite—

> Her tummy is round
> as a peach and Hikaru
> constantly glances.

The Scholar tells me
The Empress is distracted.
Her characters shake.

(Maman loves this part
of the story, God knows why—
but we repeat it!)

> Late snow melts—coo, coo!
> Two doves on two windowsills.
> In time with the moon.

Maman shuffled off down the corridor half an hour ago, I think she may have made it to the kitchen.

> From the music room
> a jangling cry rings out.
> Wolves howl in the zoo.

# DOCTOR BARBIE

Addiction's one   slippery  snake  under    a rock
Bury your  head in the sand, sure, but you put enough

Cherry Blossom up your nostrils you'll  crack!   My
diagnosis  was Denial   Dolly cared for no opinion

except her own! Hell, she was channelling  so many
figments of    Maman's imagination  Agoraphobia

germophobia,  chrometophobia—that's fear of
haemorrhaging shedloads of cash & there's no medical

intervention    for that      you can't line up for a
jab against generosity, it's not included in a First Aid

kit!  Blossom? Dolly was on it like a control group
lab rat, totally fixated—it goes back to when Andrée got

meningitis & I mean Huguette's family good as owned the
National Bank & nothing could save her  Maman's

OCD  kicked in then  She got hooked on auctions
Papa was  even worse     The Senator built a turret to

quarantine in  Bunker mentality to the max & his
Rapunzel had no Prince to save her  That's when

Spanish flu wiped out whole neighbourhoods   The
trouble with   self-made moguls is  they leave no stone

unturned   Forget TB,   Vitamin D   Poverty's the
virus! Howard Hughes, Saddam Hussein &

Wacko Jacko  Why'd they keep their  hands so clean?
X marks the spot. I know   how to scrub up    Hell

yeah!   Dolly was spiralling   You'd see her Zig-
Zag across the dancefloor  trying so hard to be happy

# LADY MAMIKO

Maman picks me up again and pops me back in the Cabbage Patch stroller. Such an inelegant vehicle. Malibu Barbie stirs in her sleep and spoons up with Squirrel Nutkin. I'm too agitated to relax, this is the third time we've made this trip. It seems she wants me to help her decide on an outfit. Maman wants to change her cardigan. I'm sure Dolly could have helped with this, she knows Maman's wardrobe better and I'm not really intimate with European dress styles. I told Maman this but she's acting like she's deaf again. She does have a hearing aid and even when she remembers to put it on I'm not sure she turns it up. Dolly has a way of terrifying the porcelains about what us dolls will do without Maman, but trust me, we'll be fine on our own. I can't seem to get this idea across to her.

I manage to steer Maman in the right direction, and we deliberately avoid passing by the TV Room where I can hear Billy Crystal and all the actors ha ha ha-ing with the Oscars orchestra music in the background, and the soft lilt of Miss Ting's laugh at one of his jokes, something about how he said he was out but he got dragged back in again. I know the feeling.

Flesh tantalises
and also disintegrates.
Meanwhile there are moths.


When we get to the foyer you need to turn right to get to Maman's bedroom, but then I realise we're heading towards the front door. We never take this route. Imagine my surprise when she stops the stroller by the hall table with another lamp with a bulb that doesn't work and starts to fumble with the lock. I can't quite believe it but she moves to open it, her tiny, skeletal frame tugging at the door in the frame until it judders suddenly open. A man who has the air and accoutrements of a doctor introduces himself, steps off the mat onto the parquet floor shaking an umbrella.

Maman insists on
a dignified exit and
perfect sunglasses.

# JAPANESE BARBIE

A simple *arigato* would've been nice—fifty
bento boxes stuffed to the brim with

Cherry Blossom is no mean feat. It was under
Dolly's bed, which meant wriggling like an

eel for what seemed like hours & yes I did
forget my fan, the one with peonies

General G gave me—so sweet, which meant I
had to go back for it because I'd've been

implicated & considering I'm not a citizen of
Japan Town, I mean I don't have family in

Kyoto or anything like that, so I rely on
Lady Mamiko, she's discreet & doesn't let

Maman's whims interfere with our parties &
now when I need her, it's dangerous & yes the

Oscars do go on, but not *forever*—Dolly's in a
panic, she's been making more spot checks &

quality-control Lab inspections, she's on the
rampage, if she finds out I was involved it'll be

*sayonara* baby. Barbieville is full of double agents
these days & it's a hundred percent gonna get

ugly if CEO Barbie doesn't get her cut, she's
vicious when crossed & she has connections

worldwide, nowhere's safe, I'll literally be
excommunicated which sucks because a million

Yen is a lot of money—I guess I'll have to be
Zen about it,  seriously,  what choice do I have?

# THE GENERAL

*Reminiscences & Recollections of General Obadiah Louverture Little Rock Yellow Bird Junior the Second*

**A MEMOIR**

*A NEW POSITION*

Sodomy, Fellatio & Cunnilingus were against the Law in 1929, as was the consumption of alcohol. This didn't stop Junior from drinking & it hardly inhibited his sex life. I awoke from a blurry dream where I was squashed between a litter of snuffling Spaniel Pups Pawing at their mother's Teats to the sounds of gasps, groans & sucking.

I recognised Harrison, Junior's beloved, by the back of his Head, which bobbed & nodded as Junior thrust his Member to the Back of his Throat. Harrison, who was dressed in a sheer silk camisole that fell slightly below his Waist was also accommodating the Cock of Viva La Vie Jolie, one of the acts at Jimmy's Backyard which had opened its front doors for the first time that night to a crowd of men in black tuxedos with green carnations in their buttonholes. Harrison was quite skewered & appeared to be in a state of ecstatic reverie. I could not discern Junior's Visage because it was clasped between the milky-white Thighs of an Actress who was sitting upon his Face & looked very much like but was not Marlene Dietrich. She wore nothing save a black leather harness & in her right Hand she held a Tom Collins.

When Junior Ejaculated it released a chain of interconnected events: as Harrison's Throat opened in receipt his Sphincter tightened, Viva La Vie Jolie shot his load & the Actress – was it Marlene? the likeness was uncanny – shifted position so as to keep Junior's Tongue at its task, she was not quite ready. Junior obliged, his Penis softening in Harrison's slackened Jaw. It always surprised me when Junior was a considerate lover because he was selfish in many other regards. Maybe it *was* Marlene?

Piano music meandered up & in through the small, circular window at the top of the room, which incidentally was the only one in the house so as to afford absolute privacy, and on which ledge I was propped. Junior had bought Harrison the Villa across the street after his brother Charles had written a beseeching letter warning of Doom, Disaster, Disgrace, Etc describing Harrison as one of those *twilight men* and *a degenerate of the Oscar Wilde type*. Junior loved that bit, reading it again to Harrison who lay with his Head on Junior's Furry chest, ice clinking in the glass as he swilled, idly, a tumbler of malt whisky—a habit Junior disliked for he felt a good Scotch should never be diluted. Harrison snorted, swiping Junior's cigarette from his hand to take a long drag—*Maybe you should make a respectable man out of me* he said staring at a flickering chink of light as it danced across the ceiling & over a rattan chair. Junior cast the letter aside with a feigned sigh *my dear, any man who marries his mistress leaves a vacancy in that position.*

Mistresses had come & gone as had wives. Junior was married & widowed twice. He had a son by the desultory name of Tertius, who wanted a respectability in his Father that Junior was neither able nor wished to provide. Monogamy was not his way, although Harrison, who was not altogether ill-suited to life within a harem, fared better than earlier extramarital prototypes. Rumours abounded: Ivy V, a Vaudeville showgirl back in that fume-filled hellhole of a hometown Butte, Montana, was eighteen, ambitious & thought she'd hit the jackpot. She came away with a legal letter & an abortion she had to blackmail Junior to shell out for. Sweet Leonie, seventeen, was another; he set her up in an apartment on West 23rd Street shortly after his second wife died. Although Leonie's primary function was to be a Beard, Junior was happy to have sex with her, alone, or with a rough Man named Gerard & or Harrison & or the Bellboy he used to make stop the elevator & get down on his Knees on the way up to his office at the Van Nuys Hotel before tipping him with a 20-dollar bill. It all depended on his mood.

Junior had a natural talent for playing one Soft-Flesh off against the other & adored the thrill of watching them Jostle & Poke in a bid for his undivided attention. Harrison & Gerard were a case in point & although he never let Harrison know, there had never really been any true competition. Gerard ended up incarcerated in a London prison, his crime I know not—Harrison was barely nineteen & Junior revelled in his luminous charms.

A string of pearl necklaces was one thing but Harrison wanted more & in lieu of diamonds Junior bought him real estate & appointed him as his Secretary, a role that later expanded to Librarian. The gifts & salary were pragmatic, but also a genuine expression of Junior's affections. Money was how he'd learnt to show & understand love. I, in my own small way, was perhaps the one exception; for I had no financial value & even after Junior's mother had me scrubbed & drubbed upon the washboard & hung out on the line to dry, my time with Yellow Bird had left more than one indelible stain upon my Person. Throughout our many years together it became increasingly hard to get through to Junior as he delved deeper into the darker realms of night. He was persecuted & pursued & persuaded into suppressing his natural desires & which, that fugitive Mindset, warped & mutated to something even I had trouble Digesting. Morality, as Oscar Wilde would have it, is simply the attitude we adopt towards people we dislike. I had warned Junior many times about exposure to his colleague Bill. To be fair, the Weasel waited until after Junior's untimely demise before publishing his vindictive & for the most part, uncannily accurate biography that was bought up & pulped by the family. He wasn't even in the inner circle, & was not, as far as I could ever make out, remotely interesting, intellectually diverse or even *fun*. He was however a good taker of notes & minutes and memoranda. He only occasionally came to the house, or socialised with Junior once they left college, but I suspect if he had done so more often we might have found him gravitating towards his spiritual home: the closet.

Forgive me, though Dear Reader, for I digress. I was a Trophy, a Token & an indispensable companion to a Child with a Father for whom nothing he did or achieved was ever good enough. Junior's own Mama died when he was thirteen, such a sensitive & Glandular age. That he still brought me to bed with him, even when he serviced himself in the manner that Adolescent-Flesh are wont to do, was evidence of how lonesome the poor Boy was in his Heart & why, in later years, he liked his life to be crowded. The only time Junior truly enjoyed being alone was amongst the fine weaves of his tailored suits that populated his capacious wardrobe, or in the elegant &

capacious library that was one of his legacy endowments. Harrison was innately stylish, the tilt of his hat reflecting the same angular structure as his cheekbones, & increasingly, as life in America became so much more harried, they spent more time in Europe, where they could relax & be a couple together.

In LA the glamour was constant & intense. For over time the Cimarron Street villa became Harrison's principal homestead before he wearied of the sheer volume of traffic & had Junior buy a new house in the Santa Monica Hills. It was one among many manoeuvres that became necessary to offset surveillance from local busybodies, AKA Pillars of the Community, who, in their deepest Hearts, would have given their right Arm & left Breast to have been invited to one of Junior's effervescent parties. Our guests at the estate on West Adams Street included Hollywood stars & starlets, moguls & maestros since long before Prohibition & the Pansy Craze. Why, Rae Bourbon was a regular & even William Dorsey Swann, the first-ever Drag Queen, former Enslaved & revolutionary Black-Flesh who had petitioned the President himself when he was imprisoned for *keeping a disorderly house* had performed at one of Junior's soirées.

Yes, his houses, for there were several—in California & latterly in Paris, were disorderly enough, but not quite in the manner that was intended by the phrase. Junior made no such profits from his curation of entertainments. As it was, Harrison's Fanny-annex was the *after after* speakeasy location, where a select few would slink past the rubber tree, across the manicured lawn & Grecian fountains of the main house to the boudoir across the road & henceforth avail themselves of every hedonistic delight that could be conjured by a Soft-Flesh whose fertile imagination was as flamboyant as his budget.

Whether it fooled anyone was debatable, but it was marginally more discreet than a midsummer orgy in the sunken garden, which brought Junior to the attention of the DA's office via a lascivious & tedious old Duffer next door who also happened to be a judge. His sense of civic duty was such that it propelled him to monitor the situation with a pair of binoculars, through which he encountered a number of artistic scenes in the manner of a Romano fresco on the Observatory balcony.

Consequently the LAPD's notorious Vice Squad had been sticking it to Junior for some time & not in the way he preferred, although one or two officers proved to be flexible enough. Particularly in the provision of narcotics. Nonetheless, many of his acquaintances & friends had fallen foul of draconian decency laws & had neither the funds nor recuperative sense of entitlement that immense wealth tends to confer on those who possess it.

William Clark Senior had been buried some four years & I had discerned a sonorous vibration deep within Junior's Being when the wizened Ferret Breathed his last; not in Junior's Heart as one might expect at the loss of a Father, but as an electric current that crackled throughout his Brain's neurological pathways to explode into a rush of Serotonin that seeped into every last Pore. Truth be enunciated, the loss of the Slobbering Snooks, a French Bulldog whose Pug-Nose & Erect Ears were a Sight I came to anticipate & dread, had Junior weeping Tears he never shed for his Kin-Flesh-Father, whom he despised for every way in which they were alike.

It is perhaps therefore instructive to relate the manner in which Junior died. It was mid-June & Junior was en route to Mowitza Lodge, his summer house in Montana. Georgie was a handsome Child & an attractive Teenager, looks he inherited from his Mother, who had come into Junior's orbit as a maid & subsequent lover. As Senator Clark had made his second wife Anna-Maman his ward when she was fifteen, Junior had plans to adopt Georgie. I found it to be a peculiar desire in both instances as their relationships were neither platonic nor paternal. Harrison at least had cut the Umbilical string.

Regardless of the best-made plans, Etc, Etc Junior suffered a Heart attack before these legalities could be enacted, due in part to his unstinting dedication to illegalities. Amongst the frisson & Genital excitements, over the years I witnessed Junior also avail himself of every recreational stimulant that might heighten his hedonistic experience. The ensuing obituaries narrated his generosity as a benefactor of the arts, an identity he was able to construct quite authentically with his elegant library & orchestra philanthropy & such like Etc. Unfortunately, Young Georgie betrayed the brevity of his seventeen years & submitted correspondence to the probate court in which Junior chastised him playfully before signing off with customary flourish. *Anyway I have a whip here & your fanny will be well spanked & you will have to eat off the mantelpiece. I love you & I kiss you with all my heart. Sincerely yours, Daddy.* The *Los Angeles Times* were more perfunctory, noting crisply that Junior had indeed *reared & educated* the lad.

Oh dear. It is by far the better option to pen one's own memoirs lest they be writ by others, or worse, the winds of Fate.

Scandal aside, it was a seismic separation on the scale of Krakatoa. Junior & I were together for fifty-seven years. We were synonymous Beings. For Harrison I fear my continuous presence in Junior's bedroom was more akin to *The Picture of Dorian Gray* where I was the physical repository onto which he projected his resentment & angst. Obviously he felt the integrity of the bond Junior & I shared. Exclusivity was something Harrison had never had & I am truly of the opinion that he found me to be some kind of rival, which was of course bizarre on multiple levels. Junior's unseemly infatuation with this young boy or that was irksome, but it was the accumulation of so many years of aggressively cultivated uncertainty, of never quite knowing, of seeing a love shimmer & shake as a mirage that might waver & disappear that did for Harrison in the end.

Junior of course paid for Harrison's time in the sanatorium—he always paid. Harrison felt discarded, wrinkled and if not useless, for Harrison was an excellent librarian, boring. It was a scenario his delicately calibrated Nervous system was insufficient to withstand. That & the Drink. & Debauchery.

Against expectation, his recovery was fairly swift & if not total, at least ample enough to deliver me, in what I considered to be a rather arbitrary & impersonal fashion (an uninsured & ill-addressed parcel in the post) into the Arms of Junior's younger sister, Huguette, who, Harrison recalled, always had a passion for dolls.

# BRAZIL BARBIE

Arriving late to the spectacular  party, I had the
benefit of very little idea     as to what kind of

cha-cha-cha carnival catastrophe I would witness!
Dollies were  everywherrre,  mannequins too & a real

elephant's foot fulllllll of umbrellas          under a
famous ballet dancer painting     Dolly says cost a

gazilllllion dollars just like she is worth more than us
Hospital life     takes place          in a plain bed

Intravenous snakes enter noses wriggle in the
jugular, writhinggggg    with healing liquids

Knives shine in the operating theatre &  I  sssshake my
lilac leg warmers    as we gather in the disco for

mambo or samba! Dolly is drunk on cachaça.
Noboddddy dares wake her, she's a moody bitch &

overrrrr the top with her *I Will Survive* bullshit
Patience wears thin, but the party must go on!

'Quick! Quick!' I glance   & I see her eyes
rolllllllll back—In Brazil, which is my country, we have

shamans, shhh shhhaking sacred maracas! I forget
that Americans don't know Amazonia medicine

unless it's      sold in    plastic baggies under a silllllllly
veil of mystery    by dealers    in stores where the

wrong music  plays!  Pan pipes!? We rollerskate at
Xanadus!       & dance lambada with moves all the

young people are doing   It is superrrr Brasiliana
zouk style & this year's most sexxxy  carnival craze!

# THE GENERAL

*Reminiscences & Recollections of General Obadiah*
*Louverture Little Rock Yellow Bird Junior the Second*

**A MEMOIR**

*GOODFELLAS VS KING KONG*

The best thing about dying young is being forever embalmed in the moist era of late adolescence. There is a gratuitous if redundant pleasure in never having to watch what once was Pert & shiny droop & dull. The worst thing about dying young is dying young. If however, one is tingling with expectation for the press of a lover's Lips, to luxuriate in summer's warmth on a stroll down Fifth Avenue where the sun casually strikes your Face, then rest assured, Death can't wait to show up.

—*Death & the Sun are two Things not to be looked upon with a steady Eye.*

I read this in the *Maxims of La Rochefoucauld.* I like this thought, although I found him to be a capital bore.

But I digress. It's the *expectation* not the arrival of Death which so troubles us. Even if our most absurd hope is that we might live forever. Edgar Allan Poe stared Death in the Eye & didn't go Blind. Death did however confiscate his Child-Bride & I do not exaggerate, Sissy as he thought fit to rename his first cousin Virginia, was thirteen to his twenty-seven when they married, which was irregular even then. Death & Poe's philandering jiggled away at her vitality as one might struggle with a faulty lock. She died of consumption in her early twenties. Her loss a sacrifice that sent the poet to the depths of oblivion & the bottle, but not to the bottom of his pit with its pendulum, for time found him capable of loving & marrying again. So too Huguette's father, the Senator.

Anna-Maman was left to wait for her fancy Man to marry her in Paris, alone with Baby Andrée & Huguette now on the way & only her Sugar Daddy's dollars wired to shield her from illegitimacy's shame.

& so it was I found myself ensconced with the surviving Brat, besieged by a growing army of Doll Drones. Compared to my time with Junior, it couldn't have been less sophisticated. The older girl was undoubtedly the more interesting although from what I could gather from Dolly's interminable tributes Andrée was riven with cliché. Like many teenagers she found Death addictive as an idea – a position that is easy to behold when every Pore of one's Body is oozing fecundity to sprout Breasts like angels' Wings.

She revelled in the macabre, as an entrée to the amuse-bouche of melancholia & even attempted to conduct a séance, reading Poe's poems from beyond the grave as channelled by a spiritualist. Huguette loitered in the doorway, uncertain, while Andrée dressed for the occasion, anointing the blackest kohl upon her eyes, parading in a velvet gypsy Cape before setting about what she believed to be the divination of her future in a quartz crystal ball.

But these trivialities, I realise, were a sham. Those who

believed her protestations as to the futility of existence she covertly despised. Those who dared express doubt she punished with a malevolent refusal to eat anything but a morsel. Little did she know that these award-worthy performances were an unconscious reaction to a divine preparation in which she would be forced to comprehend an unpalatable truth. Spirit's attempt to warn her of her destiny. You see, The Oracle may be domiciled in Delphi, but it lives within our Hearts.

If only Dolly could have known this. Her efforts have always been valiant, if misguided. That excitable Muscle may be physically absent in the cavity of her Childlike Chest, but only because she insists upon wearing it on her Sleeve! I jest. For of course a doll's Heart is inextricably linked to that of its Human. It is a vacuum which transcends matter, a mirror image, almost exact, yet reversed. & as Dolly thought she might save her beloved Maman, Huguette was convinced she could have, should have saved Andrée.   So, returning to that fateful night in March.

—Barbra Streisand ah look good ee? Dem say she ah Diva nobody cyaan compete an' dat's why she ah get to h'announce Bes' Picture. Lookee how Madonna reach Number One pon Billboard charts wit' 'Justify My Love' sexy video h'even MTV ban an' preten' she an' di bwoy deh ah call 'imself Prince of Pop ah mek jiggy-jiggy crotch-grab an *still* haffi siddung pon er seat wit no—

Miss Ting is cut short by an act of audacity committed only by the foolish or the brave. Dolly, having searched high & low for her missing Maman, runs into the room, leaps up onto a blue chenille pouffe & mounts the ebony & onyx inlaid sideboard on which the television sits, with a frenzy that is usually the exclusive domain of the desperate or possessed & proceeds with the unthinkable.

She turns the television off. In her hands she holds a microphone & speaker that together comprise an acid-tangerine karaoke set.

—Curse words explicits is no match for Samurai swords to decapitate! Dolly shrieks at the shocked assembly & most pointedly into CEO-Barbie's static face.

'Hold up there a moment Missy! Yah got dirt in them glass Eyes ah yours? Can't you see I'm on the tel-eh-*phone*?'

—'Oh, she's *always* on a call.' Astronaut Barbie tugs at the crotch of her silver spacesuit which is not the most accommodating outfit for sitting down in, then lifts the lid on her helmet's perspex visor so as to make her point more audible.—That handset was glued to her Ear in the factory, that's what makes her u-nique. Several of the Barbies snigger.

—No vinyl-face is uniques! But this is not point. Now is states of emergency. Life and deaths! Maman's Pillow Book diary intimates is disappeared. Same Louis Vuitton vanities travel bag. Also I am not finding any cherry blossom powder puff in en suite bathroom!

At this final piece of information several of the Barbies shuffle uncomfortably on the sofa where they sit together, their long tan Legs intertwined, and look steadfastly towards the TV.

—Dolly, my dear, this is getting an incy wincy bit awkward! I'm sure there's a perfectly rational explanation—let's put the television back on and we can all settle—

Swiss Barbie's attempt to ooze oil on choppy seas is met with a tsunami. Dolly hefts the portable plastic amp & speaker on to her shoulder, hurls it into their midst & shoves a manicured bonsai onto the floor, which narrowly misses the little felt tabby Muschkin who is curled in a basket below. Before anyone has time to gather their opinion on the matter Dolly leaps down & grabs Swiss Barbie by her single, Waist-length side-Plait, whirls her above her Head so her Legs gyrate like helicopter blades & flings her to the corner of the room where she hits the grey silk seaweed flock wallpaper with a smack.

—Putaine! Dolly bellows. Swiss Barbie picks herself up surprisingly quickly & stands in the corner, Hands on Hips. Of course the porcelain doll is twice if not thrice her size & despite her immaculate silk dress trimmed with starched lace, the scene that follows is reminiscent of the movie *King Kong*, where the Ape pauses to pick up a writhing Blonde in his giant, Hairy Hands. Though Dolly, in her rage & without the need to pause for cinematic effect, is swifter and scoops up her opponent, grabs her by the Neck & pulls her pretty little Head clean off her struggling Body in one deft motion.

—Saboteur attitudes such as this is *not* appreciated! Dolly is every days making maximums sacrifice. Taking saviour responsibilities to give protections. Bringing civilisations and sophisticates. & for who? All dolls. Even lowly vinyl-Faces. For what? It is maximum ungratefuls. Barbarians!

With that she strides purposefully across the room, kicking Muschkin's empty basket out of her way as she chucks Swiss Barbie's decapitated Head behind her.

Miss Ting stares at Dolly's receding Back.—T'ras'clart! Me nah tek time fuh dis kinda foolishness! Me ah go deal wit Dolly an 'er temper tantrum antic soon enuff. Why she haffi ruin h'evryting!? Come now, Miss Swiss, the rag doll bends down to peer under the sofa—let's get yuh pretty likkle Head straight back pon yuh Shoulders she says, plucking a bonsai branch out of her own tousled Hair.

—H'anyway—me wan' ketch di rest of the h'Oscars programme—*Goodfellas* mus' go win bes' picture, eh? Anyting else ah fix.

# ITALIAN BARBIE

Amore makes the world go round!
Bribery is another way to say

ciao & if that don't work The
Don gonna wanna know about it.

Evidence can be planted by a
Fifth Column: I'm from a long line of

gladiators & we're tough as the
heel of the boot! I'm colder than

ice-cream, if I have to I'll take the
jury & the judge out, drown a few

kittens. I'm modelled on Sophia
Loren, Primadonna d'Lazio:

my cleavage is a weapon the Cosa
Nostra are dying to get their hands

on, my powers of seduction made the
Pope give it up! I look like a beauty

Queen but in my heart I'm a simple
*ragazza*! Dolly's gonna sing like a

Soprano if she doesn't do business
the Italian way, you know I'm very

understanding but all the canals in
Venice couldn't make me squeal on a

wise guy, The General neither, he's an
extra special kinda fella & when

you get to know your salami from
zucchini honey, maybe we can talk.

# IRISH BARBIE

After the penny dropped it was a
bombshell for Dolly—she was up for the

craic more in the beginning—I've done
diplomatic service & her big blue

eyes were shiny with tears, c'mon get your
fiddle out, but when even a nice pint of

Guinness can't cheer you up ... she wanted
hunger strikes & city centre bombings, the

IRA, all that kinda thing, in her mind the ends
justified the means & who was I to disagree?

Kids like her, I've seen it all before, our
Liam was the same, always crying for his

Mammy, but there comes a time when there's
no more Mr Nice Guy, she wanted me to make

overtures to Mr Assistant, I said what about our
Paddy's Day, maybe she could put a few

quid behind the bar? How about one of them
Riverdance competitions? Give out a few lucky

Shamrocks? I said hadn't she had enough
troubles, believe you me, I've had my share of

unbridled shite from imperious Brits & the
Vatican. Dolly's on a crusade, waging an unholy

war, if she could just stick it to all those
xenophobic twats with their *walks into a bar* jokes.

Yeats was a genius—& there's no bloody
zed in Dublin I told her, so let's drink to that.

# MISS TING

Miss Ting Say

War inna Babylon. Nobody wan' that. Ask any beauty queen, dem preach world peace, kindness to h'animal wit big h'ambition fi save rhino, donkey sanctuary, h'open hedgehog farm—nasty, dutty creatures, that Mrs Tiggywinkle nah wash 'er undies nice—flea an' lice deh so, all kinda nastiness. H'anyways, Blossom Wars rage fi a whole heap a years. After Oscars night Dolly rip off nuff Barbie head an' threaten Samurai Sword Man a Japan Town wit' musket, fife an' drum. Miss Ting nah support gang voilence—uh uh—plenti goat kid crown 'imself King-Ram ah di Gully stink worse than John Crow batti h'only fi find 'im neck slit an' bubble in Dutch pot, where dem boil 'im hoof fi glue cos dem seh, wah tough soon get tender.

Dolly have 'er soft spot same as di rest of us. An' 'er likkle china head is di main location. Huh. All dem years she cook cherry B up inna Scientist Barbie laboratory tek a toll pon 'er mentality. Mos' a di time, is me, Miss Ting keep side eye pon ting n ting—long as di General G siddung pon 'im bureau fi scribble 'im memoirs, h'attend to mi pumpum nice an' propah, Miss Ting nah enter into it. Too much h'artist an' article roadman h'end up fi dead or good as, chain up in dungeon a bottom of Chrysanthemum Castle.

So-sos, when Japan Barbie come to me wit' special h'agenda fi end all di fuss n fight, me, Miss Ting, did prick up 'er ears Pinocchio donkey style one time. General G, 'im say 'im is special envoy broker UN-style peace talk. Me nah see dat occur yet. Cho. Ongli peace me did see 'im barter dem days was piece ah rah-rah skirt inna Barbieville Discoteque.

Y'see before Maman did reach Doctor Hospital Beth Israel Zion Train coming our way h'evry-likkle-ting did proceed according to some kinda plan, wasn't same kinda h'anarchy. Dolly mek 'er pink powder puff preparation fi cure Maman's carcinoma-nasty, which, as me did seh already, nah wuk. Maman did need sunlight an' surgical h'attention an' a hot dinner, an' fi buck up pon some soft-flesh sociability.

H'anyway, is pure joke business an' Scientist Barbie did swap up nuff pure blossom fi duplicate, look same but is a different formula. Then she lock off all di good stuff fuh 'er an' 'er fren' fi go bleach ah speakeasy nightspot 'n drive Barbie Malibu's jeep all 'bout di place like hooligan.

When Maman face still hangin' off inna jowl meet chin kinda business, Dolly get suspicious an' send two hench boss crew Jumeau, y'know dem big, porcelain dolly, move slow like sumo, a normally reside pon Texas mantelpiece or Mississippi over dem sides. Dem shake down Scientist Barbie lab and rip off nuff a di good stuff an' come like Robin Hood a Sherwood Forest.

CEO Barbie did ketch wind uh it two-twos an she send dat h'English Barbie who so and so granny is a cousin a Queen Victoria an' she tell Dolly she go tek way Dolly's By Royal Anointment fedder-crest sticker, which go halve 'er profits. By this point Dolly nuh care fi sake a h'argument, she finish up h'all 'er cherry por one massive bender so she sen' 'er likkle ribbon-n-ringlet crew f hustle-bustle a Japan Town sake bar an' gatecrash the H'Emperor Geisha party. Oiiiieeee. A pure bacchanal did folluh, but that too far inna di story, cos nex' ting Japan Barbie come sip sarsparella pon me verandah fi mek serious proposition.

Turns out Lady Mamiko did tell 'er fi go hijack Dolly's blossom stockspile from under 'er bed springs an' now Miss Mamiko live in di hospital she no 'ave no protection, so if we help 'er, she will scratch oonoo backs an' together we can flood di market, mek price plummet, end di violence an' get rich quick same time, mek nuff dollar fi me an' di General G an' find a nice likkle situation back a yard.

Firs' ting first we either haffi convince Dolly is a good idea or pay Mafia Barbie fi whack 'er. Personally, me nah check fi either a dem h'option altho' these times Dolly a troublesome as mosquito who carry dengue fever inna 'im tail. But Miss Ting is a bonafide rag doll tru n tru with special h'occasion kindness fi mek jelly trifle wobble where 'er heart woulda been. So me tell Japan Barbie fi sit tight go suck a lollypop while me tink 'bout it h'overnight, wait fi h'inspiration fi strike.

Two-twos me send Pussycat Muschkin out fi follow Japan Barbie see where she stash the blossom. Pussycat in general not di mos' loyal a Jah-Jah creature pon di ark Noah did build, but me did h'always give 'im di pink shrimp from on top di sushi Lady M use to bring crass corridor sit pon verandah an' trade news n gossips. Me nevah did say but Japan Dolly mek di prawn dem too fresh.

H'anyway General G nah reach we yard till cockcrow an 'im slide up beside me an' try fi h'act innocent. Me, Miss Ting, did mek 'im jump outta 'im skin when she turn fi face 'im an' tell 'im straight how me could smell beluga caviar an' Tatiana pussy pon im breath.

Long story short me an' di General did fuss an' fight an' next day a mek up jus' enuff fi hatch plan fi fix di situation once an f'rall. This was before Japan Barbie did fall outta di window h'onto entrance awning which did save 'er one time, tho' 'er nevah walk straight after di 'h'accident'. Fi dis reason di General did ketch fearful fi cross CEO Barbie, as 'im lieutenant out pon road an' broker dis peace a dat ... but me did remind 'im how 'im name General, Obadiah, Louverture, Little Rock Yellow Bird, an dat G is fuh General not Golly or Golliwog or any other Babylon business an' h'also how we all gonna get new h'identity like the bwoy Henry innah di Goodfellah movie. We ready for a likkle piece a peace an' quiet on h'ocean-front property inna country, drink Guinness punch an' Irish moss an' go fishin' fi hobby n leisure.

Den me did see 'im look sad an' me did remember how di General dem did like 'im dj spot Sat'dy night a Barbieville, an' mi did remind 'im how oonoo woulda had nuff cash fi h'open our own likkle dancehall, nyabingi vibez cartel. Miss Ting did also remind 'im how 'im coulda tek top spot offa Kenny Ken one time an' not haffi share limelight an always play soundclash. This did perk the General up, more me did notice than a new rocking chair.

H'anyway, two twos, as mi did h'explain already, rag mannequin softer than porcelain or plastic an' is fi dis reason di likkle-flesh dem love oonoo off so. Dis is one reason we nah tek revenge pon Dolly when she double crawss we an' General G did find 'er one Sunday mornin' pass out on di likkle piece a blossom lef' face down inna di pile like Al Pacino innah *Scarface*. Is at dis point me tell 'er fi go fin' 'er precious Maman an' see di situation inna di hospital wit 'er two likkle stare-stare dolly eye dem. She need fi go rehab, sort 'er likkle porcelain head out an' start come correct, know friend from foe, an' tek 'er tush a Barbieville mek sincere h'apology pon di karaoke PA Friday night when weekend start. She nuh like di sound a dat at all, but when she wake up fi smell di Blue Mountain coffee she a-go realise se she haffi start play ball.

# FAIRY BARBIE

Abracadabra!     And they all lived   happily ever . . .
Bollocks to that . . . I'm not gonna   sprinkle no

cheesy climax!  My mini skirt's pure butterfly wings &
dragon's  breath  When I twirl crows flee!

Enchantment's a chore   & the porcelains scrap over
fairy dust while Dolly stares at her gloomy face in the

glitterball of our sacred disco through a sequinned veil
How charming   Not! I'm sick of deathbeds

It's been umpteen years since they took Maman away
Just face the facts   But for Dolly nothing compares . . .

Kiss my tush!  Who wants to live on a ward?   It feels
like a   morgue  with all this  fucking  eternal

*mourning*  Sure, I can blow a dandelion clock, but there's
no magic formula   for bliss or contentment   Sorry to

obliterate your pretty hopes  kid! As for the handsome
prince you prayed for?   He's bewitched by an evil

Queen, a cutey called Ken who doesn't give a
rat's arse about you, so get a grip! Otherwise I'll cast a

spell that requires  at least ten thousand toads'
tongues,        a lake full of eyelashes  and twenty tons of

unicorn dung! This is a new regime   Last century's
vendettas are dusted, done!  Maman's gone & the moon

waxes & wanes again   Boo hoo, there's no letter signed
xxx?  Maman's too busy signing cheques!  She says

yes, yes  to every    wheedling request  She's in the
zone   Swaddled  in bed, happily  shaking  death's rattle!

# DOLLY

Ancient Cleopatra Queen in sedan chair to languish
dans top styles antiquities era super cool
gurney contraption is how Dolly is helping stop cruel
eye gazes on Maman's skinny face-hole just like English

Virgin Queen the Spanish Armada did vanquish
to clear all obstacles in her way! This is dutiful
bullshits merde! Up to points! Dolly receives no thanks you
from Maman who is laughing stocks again for stink trash.

Will hospital blanket Maman's face cover as Turin
shroud did shield our Lord Jesus of Nazareth?
Exaggeration, un peu. Mais if carcinoma-nasty
face-rot is gone, why is Dolly to jump in Maman's coffin?
Maman is not caring less of Dolly's most hazardous
voyage undertaken to attend hundredth birthday party.

Uninvited! At Maman's birthday party for one hundred
anniversaire Dolly is to find Maman pulling Sponge Bob
balloon string happy to giggle with money-grab
nurseys who is Dolly stuffing in bedside cupboard.

Yuks! It is absolute cheaps n nasties and Dolly is under
no obligations to listen of ten million sob
stories that trigger Maman's soft-spots to throb
with sympathies. Any simpletons would be to wonder

why stretch limousine Hummer is not made nice
for Dolly to ride in as high-class noble of Marie-Antoinette
provenance. Pah! Then it is time for birthday cake.

Disaster! Le Gateau is from corner deli with pink ice
sugars and synthetics cream with swirly Huguette
written as if first names basis is this liberty to take?

Is this liberties of charlatan soft-flesh urines to take?
Putain! Maman is dressed in flowery cotton gown
on which designer name is not printed or known.
Is not every day Maman writing thank you cheque?

Maman is paying ski-vacation for all medicines-quack
as if she is pig carcass idiot of common
street class intelligence when at home is Chrysanthemum
Castle and porcelains waiting for her return back.

It is worse situation than Lady Mamiko did explains
in cute origami notelets with calligraphy characters.
She is missing her Lady of Bonsai and our chats

on Miss Ting's verandah. Dolly makes no complain
unless there is epic and unthinkable disaster
and this when Lady Mamiko is Japanese aristocrat!

Lady Mamiko is Japan doll of aristocrat blood line
Maman did bring here by mistakes with Malibu Barbie.
Dolly is not sure this is rock-solids make-up story
but it is because of Barbie hive-mind dream times

of Hawaii surf holidays Mr Assistant did eventually find
letter of instructions (fake!!) to bring Dolly
to Maman because she is on deathbeds so sadly
missing her best friend of all porcelains however fine

or expensive and it is this humble looking creature
(This bit Dolly is not sure Mr Assistant did believe truly)
but Le Général is persuading her so she says yes

even though it is not Dolly's most obvious feature.
She is more known for her sense of funs and duty
so strong even making yoga is sensational stress.

Six AM yogas was making sensation stresses too strong
for Dolly who is trembling jelly of cold turkeys
shiver squawks after mega hectics blossom frenzy
lasting ten years plus! This is wilderness eras tristes and long.

Dolly was in down-facing black doggie-style of wrong
decisions to speak *namaste* and pretending Gandhi
peacemaker just to be friends again with enemies
who want her to make acceptance *Maman is gone.*

Cherry Blossom is best only on occasions special
and sacred and never for sorrows to drown.
This knowledge Dolly is learning in hard knocks

academy where she is unfortunates to be star pupil!
Jokes. Dolly is knowing of let go attitudes of cross-to-frown
grudges on vinyl inferiors who steals cherry stocks.

Vinyl inferiors who did steal cherry stocks is no grudges
nowdays because Dolly must go backs to our apartment
SOS ASAP to rescue *all* mannequins for future departures!
Hospital life is extremes squalors even with top budget

monnaies of super rich! Dolly is new-leaf not to judge
Maman who is splashing cash because Santa Barbara
mansion has room for all dolls including plastics and Barbies.
Rag dolls is also crème-de-la-crème important personages.

Dolly is big *namaste* grateful to Miss Ting
and of course Le Général G who did stop Dolly from
leaping upon funeral pyre as super dramatics theatrical

because she is thinking her life is not worth living
without Maman when actually Maman is having fun
with new soft-flesh best friends of Beth Israel hospital.

Pah! Even though Maman is living in Hospital Israel
Beth in New Yorks and makes maximum million dollar
donations every hour to all besties there's more
coins still in Swiss Bank and other places! It is impossible

for this monnaie to finish because capitals
with interest is immortals and Papa was robber
baron most ruthless who made Midas gold from copper
pennies and wires while poor-trash Flesh-Peoples

did die & suffers with digging & anyway American-
Africans and Jamaica peoples did makes Maman's
fortune & she must more than speak sorry to amends

make. Le Général say sames for Feather-Brave clans:
Maman must return stolen lands. Exception: Santa Barbara Mansion
where all us dolls must resides luxurious, ever and ever Amens.

# INDIAN BARBIE

Ayurveda is an ancient system,
Buddhism v Bollywood, there's no

contest, when you practise
detachment you're wise as an

elephant—if only Dolly could
forget about Maman, find a new

guru, it's heartbreaking to see her
hang on like this, she needs to burn

incense, something sweet like
jasmine & start chanting, Ha-re

Krishna, Ha-re Krishna, Krishna
loves everyone & there are other

mantras to help get through this.
Never give up!  Let laughter be the

opium of the masses, ditch the funeral
pyre vibes, seriously there's no

quid pro quo on nirvana, you can
reverse the karma sutra & ageing, it's a

shift in focus, let the light in, the
Taj Mahal is a pretty mausoleum

unfortunately the Shah & his wife had to
vacate their lives to live there,  you're

worth more than that Dolly-Jaan, our
existence is far from futile. There's a

yoga style to suit everyone & ten
zillion positions, you can do it. Om.

# LADY MAMIKO

A goose flies alone.
A goose flies in a flock, its
cries travel furthest.

# OBITUARIES AS FOUND

On 26 March, 1991
she was admitted
with     ruthless and unprincipled cancers

700 European dolls
filled out the     standard initial assessment
Unravelling Some Mystery

a 50 year-old refrigerator
'helping with her affairs'

    agreed to speak only on the condition
of anonymity
she had been managing poorly at home
– reclusive – not eating
    dolls     dollhouses were everywhere

an expert
working with pictures
          from the collection
her lip, right cheek and
right eyelid       had been pilfered

her only support system

her doctor's widow
          Doctor's Hospital
a great place for
Michael Jackson, Marilyn Monroe

Arrested development? The last child
of the Gilded Age
would live    in the hospital
for 7,364 nights

Her casket was carried up 18 steps

          A single bouquet of daisies was left.

# ACKNOWLEDGEMENTS

When I first came across Huguette Clark's obituary sometime in the summer of 2011 I read it and was rapt. Who was this mysterious heiress, who died aged 104, having lived alone in a vast New York apartment with only her dolls to keep her company? From the beginning Dolly's voice was insistent, and she didn't give up, even when I was ready to. She spoke in sonnet coronas, in a hybridised English-Doll-French I created on Google translate, and it took some time for me to realise that there were other dolls who also needed to be heard.

I am profoundly grateful to all the writers and poets and organisations that have supported me during the writing of this book. Big-up my writing buddy Malika Booker and Mimi Khalvati's seminar crew, Miriam Nash, Denise Saul and Cath Drake as well as Mona Arshi, Nathalie Teitler, Bernardine Evaristo (who posted that first Obit), Roger Robinson (who encouraged me to unleash the Barbies), Warsan Shire (maximum belligerent!), Kayo Chingonyi, Jason Allen-Paisant (for advising on Miss Ting's Jamaican); Alison McCleod at the University of Chichester; Sarah Sanders and Arts Council, England, who awarded me with invaluable time to write; Spread the Word; the UCROSS Foundation in Wyoming and the Whiting Foundation for supporting a residency and through which I was able to understand the American landscape in which the book is set; the William Clark Memorial Library, UCLA, where I was able to access research materials from the Clark family archives as a Fulbright postdoctoral scholar, and Kate Mackintosh and Fred D'Aguiar for hosting me there.

In the time since I read that first obituary, two posthumous biographies have been published about Huguette Clark: Bill Dedman and Paul Clark Newell Jr's *Empty Mansions: The Mysterious Life of Huguette Clark* and Meryl Gordon's *The Phantom of Fifth Avenue: The Mysterious Life and Scandalous Death of Huguette Clark*, which along with William Mangam's unauthorised *The Clarks: An American Volume*, were valuable research resources. I'm also deeply grateful for the serendipity of discovering that Huguette Clark's doll collection was up for auction in Santa Barbara while I was living in California (and at which I purchased the doll who became Lady Mamiko) and also for finding myself in town to coincide with the 39th International Black Doll Show at the William Grant Still Arts Center in Los Angeles.

I'd like to thank my late sister, Zoë Robinson, my first reader, and my late mother, Marie Robinson, a talented (unpublished) poet who always encouraged my writing, as well as my surviving sister Lucy and my father Ricky McCarthy, whose Jamaican patois and pan-Africanist politics infuse the characters of The General and Miss Ting.

Finally, I am grateful to Cathryn Summerhayes at Curtis Brown; Sharmaine Lovegrove, Maisie Lawrence, Hannah Chukwu, Emily Moran and Millie Seaward and the rest of the team at Dialogue for their faith and enthusiasm in the project. And finally, finally, I thank the dolls themselves, without whom none of this would have been possible.

Bringing a book from manuscript to what you are reading is a team effort.

Dialogue Books would like to thank everyone who helped to publish *Top Doll* in the UK.

**Editorial**
Sharmaine Lovegrove
Hannah Chukwu
Nithya Rae

**Audio**
Sarah Shrubb

**Contracts**
Megan Phillips
Amy Patrick
Anne Goddard
Bryony Hall
Sasha Duszynska Lewis

**Sales**
Caitriona Row
Dominic Smith
Frances Doyle
Hannah Methuen
Lucy Hine
Toluwalope Ayo-Ajala

**Design**
Hannah Wood
Jo Taylor

**Production**
Narges Nojoumi

**Operations**
Kellie Barnfield
Millie Gibson
Sanjeev Braich

**Publicity**
Millie Seaward

**Marketing**
Emily Moran

**Copy Editor**
Lynn Brown

**Proofreader**
David Bamford